SOUNDKEEPER

A Hall McCormick Thriller
By
Michael Hervey

Please visit **michaelhervey.com** for more information.

Soundkeeper Copyright 2011 by Michael Hervey

Pinckney Island map Copyright 2011 by Michael Melendez

LONELY
PALM
BOOKS

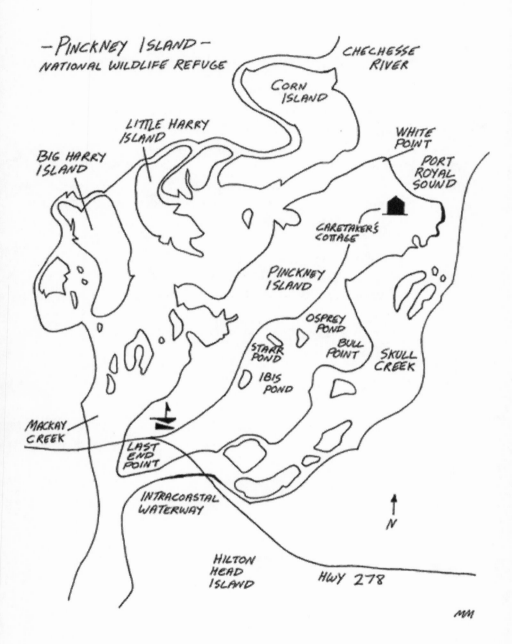

"Greater love has no one than this:
to lay down one's life for one's friends."
John 15:13
New International Version (NIV)

Chapter One

The clay-colored swirl stained the green water of Port Royal Sound and the falling tide made it easy to trace the ribbon of mud to its source. The developers of Live Oaks had been consistent with their lack of environmental stewardship so far, and she was ready to take formal action. The modest thunderstorm that had passed through the area yesterday afternoon should not have caused properly installed erosion prevention devices to fail. Gale Pickens stood on the console of her boat in order to get a better angle and balanced her leg against the windshield while she filmed with her digital video camera. When she had finished, she dipped a plastic specimen bottle into the water and collected a sample to prove that the water had enough turbidity to be lethal to certain types of sealife.

The county inspector should have been doing this, but she knew it would take him a week to return her phone call and a week after that before he made an on-site inspection. She understood how so many irresponsible developers had gotten away with so much for so long. Nobody cared, at least no one that had the power to do anything about it. But that was her job now, doing something about it, and she always did a good job.

When she finished collecting the samples she turned her boat around and let it drift with the current into the sound while she made notes to accompany the evidence she had collected. The South Carolina Department of Health and Environmental Control and the federal Environmental Protection Agency could be slow to respond to her complaints, but she had learned that they appreciated a professional and well-documented allegation. She would also provide copies of her complaint to all media outlets. They loved her videos and pictures of dirty water and pollution and usually ran teasers for her stories during reruns of CSI.

She stored her notebook and video camera in a waterproof locker and started the motor on her boat, an outboard converted to run on biodiesel. Her thoughts drifted to the going-away party she was going to tonight, and while she was happy for her friend that was retiring, she would miss him and his help. She was glad the new refuge officer had asked to take her to the party and was looking forward to seeing him again. She smiled when she thought about his lopsided smile and shy demeanor.

With a tug of the wheel she corrected her course to head home, and when she rounded the point of St. Phillips Island she was surprised to see a barge anchored near the shore. The ship had more rust than paint on its hull and didn't have a name on it, just documentation numbers sprayed on the side. Most of the boat traffic stayed in the Intracoastal Waterway, and Port Royal Sound had little commercial shipping this close to the open ocean. She angled closer and noticed that the boat was listing to its port side and the engine wasn't running. She wondered if the boat was aground and noticed a sheen on the water near the stern.

"Hello!" she called out as she pulled alongside. The deck of the barge was several feet higher than her boat. No one answered, so she called again.

"Hello!"

She tied her boat to the railing of the barge and pulled herself aboard. The fuel leaking into the water was a major problem, but her first concern as a mariner was that everyone on board was alright. As soon as she hoisted herself over the railing she realized that she had misidentified the vessel. It was not a typical cargo barge but a hopper barge, the type of boat that usually worked in conjunction with a dredge. When a dredge was used to deepen a channel, the mud and sand that was collected from the bottom of the waterway, referred to as spoil, was loaded onto the barge and taken out in the ocean to a designated area to be unloaded. The hull of the hopper barge had massive underwater doors so the materials would fall out of the bottom of the boat when the doors were opened.

Gale noticed the cargo area was full of copper-colored dirt, not sand and mud. This soil was from inland, which was very unusual. The wind shifted and chemical fumes stung her nose.

"Hello!" she called again. The door leading from the pilothouse was open and she stepped inside.

"Is anybody here?"

"Who's there?" The voice was gruff and unpleasant. Before she could answer, the owner of the voice climbed out onto the deck from a hatchway.

"What the hell are you doing on my boat?" he demanded.

The man was short and wide. His forearms looked like Popeye's and were covered with so many blurry and faded tattoos that it was impossible to discern any one image. His large, thick hands were greasy, and he held a wrench in one of them. Gale noticed his stained teeth when he asked again what she was doing.

"I thought you might need some help," she said.

"We don't need any help."

Whoever he was, he wasn't local. His accent was from north of the Mason-Dixon Line.

Gale hadn't seen anyone else on board, but the unseen voice of another man called out. "Who are you talking to?"

A second man climbed out of the hatch. He was wearing jeans and a plaid golf shirt hanging off his shoulders. His spiked hair was bleached blonde and dark eyebrows looked mismatched above his pock-marked nose. His eyes locked onto hers.

"I just wanted to make sure that you were okay. I thought you had lost your engine and were aground."

"That's very considerate of you," the blonde one said. He smiled at her and she felt goosebumps rise when he leered at her legs, and she realized he knew she was alone. He wanted her to know he was looking at her.

"Soundkeeper," he said, reading the name of her boat. "Environmental watchdog, right?"

Gale knew she was in trouble. She felt real fear for the first time in her life. Her pulse was racing and her peripheral vision narrowing. These long-bred survival instincts were pulling blood from her extremities into her core, preparing for a fight.

"People know where I am." Gale took a step toward the nearest railing, but Blondie mirrored her motion, cutting her off. He smiled at her again, put his hand in his pocket and took a step closer to her. Another step and he was within arm's reach. When his switchblade flicked open, she kicked him in the balls as hard as she could.

Blondie was down and groaning before Gale reached the line securing her boat. She threw one long leg over the railing when a greasy hand clamped over her mouth and she was pulled backward off of her feet. She tasted blood and grease when she bit down as hard as she could and heard the tattooed man curse. His hands dropped to her waist and he squeezed her so tightly she couldn't breathe.

She stopped struggling when she saw the blade of the knife dancing in front of her eyes.

The sick smile had disappeared from Blondie's face. He was in obvious pain.

"Bitch," he spat through clenched teeth and slapped her with his open palm. Gale tasted blood again, hers this time. She saw him draw back and the last thing she saw before the blackness was a rusty wrench, arcing toward her head.

"Get us out of here and head out to sea," Blondie said to the tattooed man. He bent over, grimacing. "We'll cut her boat loose and dump her with the dirt."

Chapter Two

Hall McCormick was on the water an hour before the first tangerine slices of light tickled the eastern horizon. He picked up Jimmy Barnwell at the boat landing and together they headed across Calibogue Sound to begin their last day together.

Refuge Law Enforcement Officer Hall McCormick, of the U.S. Fish and Wildlife Service, had worn his uniform for only twelve weeks. The waters he was navigating were as new and unfamiliar to him as his uniform and the thought of losing his trainer and guide had kept him from sleeping most of the night. When Jimmy Barnwell retired today at the end of their shift, he would take twenty-five years of experience with the agency and fifteen years of local knowledge with him. Other than Hall, the nearest refuge officer was stationed miles away at the Savannah refuge.

In the middle of the sound Hall cut the motor on the patrol boat and plopped down on the seat. He stared out toward the placid ocean and wondered how long it would take the tide to push them back behind the island. Jimmy put a fresh plug of Red Man in his mouth and spit a stream of tobacco juice over the gunwale before he spoke.

"You'll do alright boy," the older man said in his quiet voice. The younger man seemed unconvinced.

"When is the next full moon?" Jimmy asked.

"A week from Tuesday," Hall replied.

"How many bass under eighteen inches can you keep?"

"None."

Jimmy smiled and spit again.

Every day for the past two months had been a learning experience for Hall McCormick. With a graduate degree in marine biology he came to the job knowing intimate details about the life cycle of the Sciaenops ocellata, or spottail bass as the locals called them, but virtually nothing about the laws that protected them and their environment. Jimmy provided no textbooks for his course. He quizzed his student every day on matters ranging from federal fisheries regulations to South Carolina game laws. The practical courses were even tougher: boat handling, course plotting, and vessel safety checks.

Twice Hall had failed in the field. Hall ran their boat aground on Brams Point after being told the day before that the shoal there was too shallow to cross at anything less than three-quarters of the high tide. Hall's pride was damaged but the boat was not. It was easily freed from the mud and the lesson was ingrained forever. The second failure drew much more criticism from his teacher.

Two weeks ago they stopped a small runabout for suspicion of boating while impaired. Hall failed to notice a handgun in the glove box of the boat when the young man operating the craft retrieved his registration papers. With his hand on his pistol Jimmy told the young man to keep his hands where he could see them and deftly stepped over to the other vessel. The gun was legal and the owner was just distracted, not drunk. He was sent on his way with some advice about operating his boat in a safer manner.

"Most people you run into are good folks, even the ones you have to cite or take to the magistrate. Every once in a while you'll run into someone who's not so nice and doesn't think much of that uniform you're wearing. That's why they gave you a gun to go along with the badge," Jimmy had told him.

It was the gun Hall hated more than anything else about his new job. After graduate school, he tried to get a job with every state fisheries agency east of the Mississippi, but with no success. No one was hiring marine biologists. There were positions open but lean budgets meant non-critical personnel who left or retired were not being replaced. The federal agencies weren't hiring biologists either but they were hiring law enforcement officers.

He never took the idea of being a "fish cop" seriously until he was still unemployed eight months after he received his master's degree. Both of his roommates had moved out and his landlord was pressing for another year's lease. He liked his job at the marina because he was outdoors all day, but minimum wage wasn't going to pay the rent, the grocer, and the college loans too. So instead of peering through a microscope trying to find a way to kill the pfisteria organism, he went to Glynco, Georgia for eighteen more weeks of school. He trained to become a law enforcement officer and resolved to get a job where he could use his education as soon as possible.

While at the Federal Law Enforcement Training Center, FLETC, he took classes in evidence collection and case preparation, surveillance techniques and self defense and weaponry. At a lean six feet two inches tall and 210 pounds Hall easily passed the self defense classes, and four years of intramural rugby hadn't hurt his physical conditioning at all. Carrying a gun wasn't a big deal for him. He had grown up hunting with his father and uncles and was satisfied with his ability to defend himself, but the heavy gun on his side was a constant reminder of his unfulfilled dream.

Over the past eight weeks Jimmy had gotten very good at guessing what Hall was thinking. Today was no exception.

"I didn't want this job when I took it twenty-five years ago. I never thought I'd retire from the service."

Hall was surprised. After working with him for two months, he couldn't imagine Jimmy Barnwell as anything but a game warden. He thought the man had been born to be a federal wildlife officer. From how he talked with the commercial fishermen to the way he taught a hunter safety course to teenagers, Jimmy was a professional.

"I needed a job and the wildlife service was hiring a lot of vets. I wanted to be a helicopter pilot and fly roughnecks out to the oil rigs. By the time I'd saved enough money for flight school, I finally realized I loved my job. I'm just glad I realized it before I quit."

Hall wondered how much of the story was true and how much of it was the father in Jimmy coming out. Either way it didn't make him feel much better. Tomorrow he would be out here by himself, with too much to remember and no one to ask for help.

"Head over to Skull Creek. I promised Gale I'd stop by today."

Skull Creek wasn't really a creek at all, just a sliver of water separating the northeastern end of Pinckney Island from Hilton Head Island. Pinckney Island, the whole of which was taken up by Pinckney Island National Wildlife Refuge, existed in anonymity in comparison with the larger Hilton Head Island. The average visitor to Pinckney Island stayed less than forty-five seconds, the amount of time it took to cross the narrow island on the Highway 278 causeway at sixty-five miles an hour on the way to the resorts for golf or tennis. Over 300,000 visitors a year visited the refuge to go hiking, bird watching, and enjoy their public lands.

Hall's job was to patrol the 4,053-acre National Wildlife Refuge and enforce federal fisheries regulations, assist the Coast Guard with search and rescue missions, oversee controlled deer hunts, and catch offenders who committed violations ranging from speeding and littering to poaching and killing endangered species, and a million other responsibilities, or so it seemed. It was far too overwhelming to consider everything at one time. But Hall was determined to do a good job because it would ensure a good recommendation when he applied for the next biologist vacancy. His boss, Susan Charles, was the refuge manager, a biologist and former refuge officer herself before she climbed the ladder and took herself out of the field and away from the lab.

They entered the no-wake zone in Skull Creek and Hall brought the boat down off plane and idled up to the old wooden docks of Low Country Seafood, ramshackle and in need of repair. Hall preferred the neat concrete docks of the new marina just a mile upriver to the smelly fish house, but the marina was too pricey for the environmentalist they were going to see. Shelby Pickens, the owner of Low Country Seafood, was sympathetic to the conservation cause and offered cheap office space and a free boat slip. It also helped that the Soundkeeper happened to be his daughter.

Jimmy Barnwell had never heard of a Soundkeeper until Gale Pickens tied her boat up to his dock one day last year and introduced herself. She had been hired as the Soundkeeper for Port Royal Sound and the surrounding watershed by a partnership of private conservation groups. As soon as she explained to him that Soundkeepers, Riverkeepers and Waterkeepers were in place across the country and around the world combating water pollution and protecting fragile wetlands, Jimmy accepted her as an ally. Rarely a week had gone by in the past year that they had not been in contact with one another. Jimmy taught her how to collect evidence that would be admissible in court and Gale passed on tips about lawbreakers that her "Coastwatchers" provided when they didn't want to get involved. They stopped being business associates and became friends many months ago.

Hall eased up to the docks slowly, having not yet mastered the ability to approach at cruising speed and shift into reverse just in time to stop without slamming into the dock. He was looking forward to seeing Gale and was taking her to Jimmy's retirement party tonight. They had gone out a few times, twice for dinner and once on a Saturday to pick up litter together with some of her volunteers. He didn't know if that counted as a date but he hoped it did. Gale was a cutie, petite with toned runner's legs and a ponytail the color of Carolina beach sand. Her tan was dark and natural and he liked the fact that she seemed like a real person, unlike so many girls he had known in college and grad school.

They walked into her small office and Hall surveyed the "foxhole," as he'd heard Gale refer to it. A huge map of Port Royal Sound took up one wall of the small room. On another wall was a "Ten Most Wanted" list, and on it were written the top environmental offenders in the Port Royal Sound watershed. The group included golf courses, developers, and three unidentified polluters. The numbers beside their names corresponded to dots on her large map and they were spread throughout the area.

On her desk, beside the latest issue of Sierra magazine was a mason jar full of shark's teeth, and a tube of toothpaste. The number eight blinked on her answering machine. Hall knew she lived above her office in a small apartment and thought that he caught a whiff of bacon, a thought that made his stomach growl, loud enough that Jimmy looked at him with a raised eyebrow.

"Gale, I filled up your tank." Someone else was coming in the front door.

A white guy with greasy dreadlocks and a tie-dyed t-shirt with a picture of Bob Marley on it stopped when he saw the two uniforms. The bacon Hall thought that he smelled was now overpowered by the scent of incense and stale marijuana.

"I don't think she's here, Stanley." Jimmy said.

"Cool, no problem Dude. I'll leave her bill on the desk." Stanley put a piece of brown grocery bag with some numbers written in magic marker on her desk and backed out the door, almost bowing to the two officers.

"I didn't know there were any hippies on Hilton Head." Hall said after he'd left.

"At least one. Stanley makes biodiesel from old cooking oil, and house sits for absentee owners. I guess they think he's helping them reduce their carbon footprint since it's easier to buy a clean conscience than to change your lifestyle. Let's go get some breakfast.

Chapter Three

Her father had named her Gale after a hurricane washed out the road to their home the day she was born, and she spent the first month of her life in a house without electricity or running water. Her dad ran the family seafood business that his grandfather had founded, and owned half a dozen shrimp boats that fished the waters surrounding Hilton Head Island. She grew up visiting him almost every day at the docks, climbing all over the boats and going out on the water before she was old enough to walk. She started racing in Sunfish regattas in the Beaufort River when she was ten years old and worked at the city marina through high school, commuting in her own little Boston Whaler. On her nineteenth birthday she sailed out of Beaufort on the Island Mercy, a volunteer on the hospital ship that took her to five of the earth's seven seas. In her entire life she had never been more than fifty miles from the ocean.

She awoke disoriented and hurting, but comforted by the gentle rise and fall of a boat on the water. She was thirstier than she had ever been in her life. Her eyes were heavy and she felt herself slipping away again, the ache in her head pounding with every heartbeat. It was dark and hot, wherever she was. A tarp had been thrown over her and the gasoline fumes were suffocating her. She'd peed in her pants. She heard a voice she recognized and her pulse hammered even faster.

"By the time I get back, all that dirt and the bitch better be at the bottom of the ocean. Do you think you can handle that, Arnold?"

Just before she passed out again Gale heard someone sobbing, just loud enough to be heard over the clattering boat engine and the hiss of the water against the hull. It scared her even more when she realized the crying she heard was her own.

The tattooed man grunted but didn't look up from the stubborn hydraulic pump he'd been working on for the last several hours. He hadn't yet figured out why it refused to work properly and open the bottom of the boat like it was supposed to.

"I'll tell our client why we can't take any more dirt until tomorrow," Blondie said. He eased onto the rickety dock to avoid bumping his severely bruised testicles. "Don't screw up again, Arnold."

Arnold didn't make another sound until four hours later when he found a small hole in the hydraulic line that led from the pump to the cylinder that operated the opening mechanism. A clean bilge would have made the leaking fluid easy to spot, but Arnold neglected the boat even worse than he neglected his personal hygiene.

With the barge operating properly, or at least as good as it was going to, Arnold left Cole's Landing and chugged down the Broad River and into Port Royal Sound. He turned on the VHF radio to see if anyone had found the troublemaker's boat. So far, so good it seemed. There was no chatter on the radio about a missing boater. They had cut her boat adrift five miles out to sea and tried to dump the contaminated soil, but the hopper doors wouldn't open and Blondie wanted to dump the girl and the dirt at the same time. Now Arnold was alone with all of the evidence, which he would blame squarely on his partner if he had the misfortune of getting stopped. The last felony he was involved with had cost him ten years of his life and he didn't plan on a repeat engagement. The cops were always eager to bargain away a bird in hand for one in the bush which was why he had been a guest of the state of South Carolina for only ten years instead of twenty.

The old barge handled the small ocean swells poorly, giving the man at the helm the first qualms of seasickness. Two miles out was far enough, he reasoned. He didn't know how to swim and he spent too many hours watching Shark Week on the Discovery Channel to want to have anything to do with the water. Arnold undid the safety catches and was about to release ten tons of contaminated soil into the ocean when he saw the bright blue tarp that Blondie had covered the body with. He knew it wouldn't sink and would be easy to spot in the water, so he reset the safety latches and climbed across the greasy dirt to retrieve it.

After he pulled the tarp off the body the open, hazel eyes of the dead woman were the second thing that Arnold noticed, the first being her terribly swollen jaw. Then the dead eyes blinked.

He cursed and fell backwards into the dirt, smacking his head on a railing on his way down. He scrambled back to her and her eyes were closed again. He thought that he'd imagined her eyes opening but then he watched her chest rise and fall.

She was still alive. Getting rid of a body that someone else killed wasn't a big deal for him. Neither was sticking an unloaded gun in somebody's face for their wallet. Killing someone, especially a woman, was something else entirely. And if she was alive when he dumped her in the ocean he knew he would be the one who killed her and he couldn't live with that. He was a thief, a robber, a liar, and an addict but he would never hurt a woman. His mother had raised him better than that.

Without any idea of what he was going to do with her, Arnold carried Gale into the pilothouse, duct-taped her arms behind her back, and tied her legs around a pipe. He didn't even notice she'd wet her pants. Once she was tied up, he undid the safety latches again and pulled the lever. The barge shuddered and jumped several feet higher in the water as the dirt left the cargo bay. Arnold didn't notice a dolphin surface nearby and watch him for a moment before it swam away. He didn't see the school of mullet that was poisoned or the larval jellyfish that the tainted soil melted into the mud. Two mature cobia, swimming in formation with a large manta ray, swam through the toxic cloud and when the tainted water spread over their gills it seared their lamellae and sent them to the bottom of the sound. The slick spread out into the ocean and deeper into the water on the retreating tide and killed for miles and miles.

Halfway back to port the girl began to regain consciousness, so Arnold covered her eyes with an oily rag. He noticed how pretty she was and wondered if he could keep her, at least for a little while. Blondie never went into the old fish house. Maybe he could hide her in there, at least until his dealings with Blondie were over. Maybe by then he could show her that he wasn't such a bad guy. After all, he'd just saved her life. A little gratitude would be in order.

Chapter Four

Although she was blindfolded, Gale knew she was back in familiar waters by the ripe smell of the marsh at low tide, which meant it was late afternoon. Her hands were taped behind her back, and her legs were tied to something. Fear and helplessness gathered in her throat, and she fought the urge to cry. The boat bounced off of something solid and the noisy engine shut off. She tensed when she heard someone approach.

"If you try to get away or anything, I'm going to let my friend cut you up. Do you understand?"

Gale nodded. She recognized the voice of the tattooed man. The one she had bitten.

"If everything works out, you'll be just fine," he said.

She stiffened when she felt his rough hands on her bare legs. His body odor was overpowering, and she realized he was stronger than she had given him credit for when he carried her off of the boat and walked several minutes without even breathing hard. She turned her head away from him and tried to look underneath her blindfold but couldn't see anything. Old boards creaked and moaned, the light dimmed, and she heard a door close. Arnold took off her blindfold.

"Jeez, your mouth is really swole up," he said.

The pain that had been blocked by fear crept back to the surface. Opening and closing her mouth, she was relieved when she didn't hear any grinding and popping and that none of her teeth were loose. If her jaw was broken, it wasn't severe. She knew from her years on the hospital ship that a fractured jaw was most often left to heal itself. A crooked smile was the least of her concerns. She was dizzy and sick to her stomach, symptoms of a concussion. She held her breath as Arnold stomped over to her and slipped the blindfold back over her eyes. His gentleness scared her.

"Don't move," he ordered.

Gale felt the vibrations as he walked away and guessed that she must be in a building that was built on pilings above the marsh. Her hands were still tied behind her back, but her feet were free and she stood up. She counted her steps as she walked toward light that penetrated her blindfold. When she bumped into the wall she rubbed her blindfold against the wall until she could see and peeked out of a partially boarded up window. Any hope of calling for help vanished when she saw miles of empty marsh beyond the dilapidated dock.

She looked around and realized she was in an old, abandoned fish house. The walls were made of rough wood, but the wooden floors were polished smooth from decades of commerce. The roof was tin and had rusted through along one edge. There were double doors large enough for a truck on one end of the building and a commercial ice maker that looked like it had been stripped for parts. No lights were on, but there was a television, a cot and a lawn chair in one corner of the building. A small closet was built into one of the walls, but other than that the entire space was wide open.

She felt footsteps and tiptoed back to where she had been. She wiggled her nose and the blindfold fell back in place just as she heard the door open. Arnold untied her hands and took her blindfold off again.

"Here," he said. He handed her a plastic bag with ice.

Gale nodded and put the cool bag on her swollen jaw. Then she noticed what else he was carrying.

"I'm going to have to make sure that you don't go anywhere, at least until after we're done."

The cold steel ratcheted around her ankle.

"Is it too tight?" he asked. She wanted to scream, but just shook her head.

He walked around the room, measuring a heavy chain as he went. When he seemed satisfied he looped the chain over a steel girder that had once been used to hoist heavy loads of shrimp and crabs onto trucks.

"If my partner finds out that you're alive, he'll kill you, understand?"

Gale nodded.

"Maybe when we're done I can let you go."

It was the first time she felt hopeful since she had been kidnapped. She had to clear her throat several times before she could speak.

"Done with what?" she asked.

Chapter Five

N ear Big Harry Island they stopped to watch a pair of biologists pull a seine through the shallow water of the mudflats. Comfortable in T-shirts, fishing waders and ball caps, they were accompanied by a research assistant Hall recognized. She was recording the number and size of the horseshoe crabs they netted on a clipboard, and she smiled and waved to them as they passed by. The biologists were conducting surveys to make sure the population of horseshoe crabs wasn't declining. Hall knew enzymes from the blood of horseshoe crabs were unique in the animal kingdom because of their ability to fight pathogens and infections and were being used in cancer research. Hall gave them a longing look before he waved back and sped away.

Parris Island was quiet on their starboard side when they passed by. Hall had passed by the Marine Corps training depot many times before and usually heard the sounds of gunfire or cadence being called by the drill instructors as they worked their recruits. Hall had an uncle who was a Marine, and all he remembered about Parris Island was the heat and the mosquitoes. He had been kind enough to pass this information on to Hall just before he left for neighboring Pinckney Island and Hall had the insect bites to prove his uncle had been right.

The municipal marina was next to a waterfront park with a bandstand and behind the park was a small downtown area. Beaufort was the second oldest city in South Carolina and most of the buildings having been built in the previous century, had been well preserved or restored. The old construction methods of tabby brick and rough pine boards was still visible on many buildings, and horse-drawn carriages pulled tourists under live oaks and magnolias that shaded the park and antique shops. The diner here offered shrimp and grits long before the dish was served at any trendy bistro.

Along the seawall were several porch swings hanging from pergolas, the perfect place to while away a lazy afternoon and make it feel like being in a hurry was a crime. Further down Bay Street was the U.S. District Courthouse. It was close enough to walk to from the Marina, which Hall and Jimmy had done more than once, and he wouldn't have been surprised if they saw Forrest Gump or the Great Santini walking along Bay Street. Being in Beaufort reminded Hall of all the neat seaside towns his family had vacationed in when he was a kid.

The Rebecca Ann was moored at the end of one of the piers at the city marina. Hall let Jimmy take the wheel of the patrol boat, not wanting to misjudge the current and put the first blemish on the new paint. Jimmy's wife Rebecca heard them coming and waved as she came out onto the deck of the sailboat. Jimmy waved back and eased up alongside his new home without effort, judging the current and wind with practiced expertise.

Hall liked Jimmy's wife a lot and smiled at her as he climbed aboard. When Rebecca Barnwell had found out that Hall would have to live in a hotel for eight weeks until she and Jimmy vacated the caretaker's cottage on Pinckney Island, she decided they would move onto the Rebecca Ann before it was finished. Hall once again admired the fit and finish of the Rebecca Ann. He knew that Jimmy and Rebecca had done most of the work themselves, turning the derelict ketch into a vessel worthy of live aboard cruising. The Barnwells were going to follow spring all the way up the coast to Maine and spend the summer exploring the coves and beaches of the New England coastline.

"There's still a problem with the radar," Rebecca said after Jimmy poured himself a cup of coffee. She handed Hall a thick sausage biscuit. Grease spots soaked through the napkin it was wrapped in. He thought it was the best thing he had tasted in months.

"Are they coming to fix it?" Jimmy asked.

"He's supposed to be here before noon," she answered.

Jimmy looked at his watch and smiled.

"I've decided to take early retirement," he announced.

Hall felt the blood rush from his face in panic, and he coughed on a piece of sausage. He had been counting on six more hours of instruction. Companionship.

"Don't look so worried, Hall. You'll do fine," Jimmy told him.

Hall stayed as long as could but decided to leave before the tide was completely gone. He wanted to go back to his house before lunchtime and thought the safest thing for him to do was stay at home and catch up on his paperwork. The channel that led to his dock could be tricky at low tide, so he reluctantly said his good byes and cast off.

The wind was against him as he crossed Port Royal Sound, and he put on his rain slicker to keep the spray from drenching him. The small, open boat offered little protection from the elements. Between the noise from the wind and motor and the concentration required to keep the boat on course in the choppy water the voice on the VHF radio had hailed him three times before he realized he was being called.

"This is the refuge officer," Hall said into the microphone. He still wasn't comfortable talking on the radio and slowed the boat so he could hear.

The woman who was calling him reported a dolphin in distress in the May River near Bluffton. She said that it was tangled in a fishing net and looked like it was dying. After checking his chart, Hall gave the caller his ETA and corrected his course. Along the way he heard someone from the Waddell Mariculture Center on the radio. They were responding as well, and Hall hoped they got there first since they were the primary responders for beached whales, injured sea turtles, and the like. He was concentrating so hard on his navigation, watching the channel markers and buoys, that he didn't realize until he arrived that he had no idea of what to do for a dolphin in distress.

Three boats were rafted together and drifting in the current: a big sportfishing yacht, a motorsailer with its sails furled, and a large Zodiac inflatable boat. The Zodiac belonged to Nature's Way, an ecotourism company from Hilton Head that specialized in dolphin watching cruises. Near the boats he saw a large dolphin struggling on the surface. She did not remind him of Flipper.

With some skill and more luck he managed to tie his boat to the others without scattering them like billiard balls.

"I think she's tangled in an old fishing net, Officer," a blue-haired lady on the motorsailer said. She must have been the one who called him, and Hall reminded himself to thank her later. The dozen or so people on the dolphin cruise were alternately videotaping him and the dolphin, clearly waiting for him to do something. He hoped Jimmy was having just as much fun trying to get his radar fixed.

Hall's knowledge of bottlenose dolphins or porpoises was very limited. He knew they were intelligent and very social animals. He also knew that their mouths were lined with razor sharp teeth and remembered when he was a kid he had seen a dolphin at Seaworld launch a woman all the way across a large swimming pool.

They were also protected by the Federal Marine Mammal Protection Act, a direct responsibility of the U.S. Fish and Wildlife Service, Hall's employer.

"I'm going to try and snag her and pull her over to the shallow water near the shore. It will be much easier to free her there," Hall announced with more enthusiasm than he felt. The tourists on the Zodiac nodded in approval and no doubt believed Hall handled all of his dolphin rescues in that manner. Hall untied the line from his anchor and coiled the rope in preparation to throw. He hoped the rope would catch on the rough surface of the net, but after the third try it was apparent that it would not.

The dolphin began clicking and squealing, which solicited sympathetic "Oohs" and "Ahhs" from all of the spectators. Hall was just getting ready to call Jimmy for help on his cellular phone when a small fishing boat with a huge outboard motor idled up and joined their flotilla. The bearded captain talked to the woman on the motorsailer for a moment and then pulled off his shirt and slipped into the water. He swam towards the dolphin, and Hall saw him whisper to her. To Hall's amazement, the dolphin stilled as if she understood what the man was going to do. Treading water, the man used a small knife to cut away the net.

"I need another hand," the man in the water said, looking at Hall.

Hall unbuckled his gunbelt, took off his shirt and body armor and was down to his boxers before he had time to think about what he was doing. He slipped over the side of his boat into the cool water.

"I can't reach all the way around her and hold the net at the same time," the man said. Hall positioned himself on the other side of the dolphin and swam close to her, waiting for a flick of her powerful tail fluke to snap his neck.

"Easy girl," Hall said. Her giant eye looked right at him, and he touched her for the first time. Her skin was smooth and warm, just like his, and there was a long pink scar in front of her blowhole. He stroked her side with one hand and lifted the net over her dorsal fin with the other. Within a few seconds the dolphin swam free and disappeared. She surfaced a few yards away and performed a jump worthy of an amusement park show. Then she was gone.

Cheers and applause echoed from the other boats and Hall swam back to his patrol boat. Someone from the motorsailer tossed a towel to him and he dried off.

"You must be taking Jimmy's place," his fellow rescuer said. He was back on his own boat now.

"I'm Hall McCormick."

"Silas Pickens," he said. "Nice to meet you."

"Gale's brother?" Hall asked.

Silas Pickens nodded and waved as he motored away, and Hall almost called out to ask for his number, when he saw the name of his boat: Native Son. No need for a phone number. He would be able to reach Silas on the radio if he ever wanted to talk to him.

Hall managed to make it through the shallow channel leading to his dock without getting stuck in the mud. With most of the water drained from the creek, the marsh smelled heavy, a combination of salt and decay, although the decay nurtured new life. Detritus, created by the decaying marsh plants, nourished small animals and became the foundation for the salt marsh food chain. Innumerable marine species called the marsh home for either all or part of their lives. Blue crabs, shrimp, oysters, even some of the pelagic fishes like barracuda lived through their larval stages and into adolescence in the protective haven of mud, grass, and water.

Dozens of male fiddler crabs waved their comically disproportionate white claws from the muddy shoreline, trying to get the attentions of potential mates. Hall smiled to himself as he tied up his boat and pounded across the old wooden dock toward the house.

His "new" home had been a hunting cabin back when the island was privately owned. A single-story wooden structure, it was built only seven feet above sea level, which meant that several hurricanes and a few unnamed storms had flooded it with their surging waters. It was not air-conditioned, and Jimmy and Rebecca had taken their window unit with them for their sailboat. Hall hoped he would be able to afford a replacement before summer. He was looking for some dry underwear when his telephone rang.

"There's a fish kill on the north side of Port Royal Sound," the caller said. Hall questioned her and found out she was one of the volunteers that worked with Gale Pickens as one of her Coastwatchers. She had tried to reach Gale on the Soundkeeper Hotline but no one had answered so she called Hall for assistance. The lady explained that she was out for a day cruise with her granddaughter when they saw several hundred dead fish floating near the mouth of a creek that fed into the sound.

"Can you describe your surroundings so I can find you?" Hall asked. He unrolled a chart on the kitchen table that doubled as his desk.

"How about the exact latitude and longitude?" the grandmother asked.

Hall wrote down the coordinates in his notebook and told her he would be there within half an hour. He stuffed a granola bar in his pocket and grabbed a bottle of water before he headed out the door.

Chapter Six

The chain allowed Gale to move through most of the warehouse. She couldn't reach the window or door, but could have walked over to where Arnold was sitting if she had wanted to. Her only furniture was a lawn chair with half the seat rotted out. Neither she nor her captor had spoken in several hours. Arnold seemed entranced by Wheel of Fortune and Jeopardy! Gale was ignoring the television, concentrating hard to manage the pain in her jaw.

"Are you hungry?" Arnold asked.

Gale nodded her head. Fear paralyzed her when Arnold walked toward her, his steps vibrating through the elevated building. To her great relief, he only checked the handcuff on her ankle and the chain it was connected to. He left without saying another word.

Outside a small outboard boat motor sputtered for a few seconds then coughed to life. She had seen it moored beside the barge and now it gave her hope. If she could get free from the chain, it was a way of escape. A small boat motor didn't need a key to start.

Gale began to examine the rusty chain and the steel beam it was attached to, determined to find a way to escape. "Dear Lord," she thought, "please don't let this place catch on fire!" She reminded herself how tough she was, how she had always prided herself on her ability to overcome adversity. She soon realized that although the chain was old and rusty, it was more than adequate to keep her imprisoned. Her hands were covered with rust from the chain and ached from pulling and tugging on it. For some reason she thought of Hall and wondered if he was looking for her and wondered if anyone at all was looking for her now. Her tears trickled at first, then came in a convulsion of silent, heaving sobs.

By the time Arnold returned, Gale had regained her composure and checked her watch. He had been gone for forty-five minutes and walked in with two grocery sacks and a bag of ice. He put the ice in a cooler along with a six-pack of Budweiser. Then he handed her the grocery bags.

"I got you a few things," he said.

Arnold opened a beer and turned the television back on. Gale investigated the contents of the bags.

The first thing she checked was the receipt, hoping that it named the store and gave its location. She was disappointed to find that it was a plain, white register tape that simply noted the price of each item and the total. She put it in the pocket of her shorts. Evidence, she hoped, for an upcoming kidnapping trial.

The bags were full of groceries, mostly canned soups and meats. She brightened when she realized that Arnold wasn't going to kill her anytime soon, but was too scared to think about why he was keeping her alive. Maybe he would let her go eventually.

She opened a can of Spam and used the sharp edge of the lid to cut it into slices. She wondered if it was sharp enough to cut a man's throat and then wondered if she was strong enough to go through with something like that. She wasn't sure, but hid the lid in the bottom of the grocery sack.

It was the first food she had eaten since two slices of bacon before dawn and she didn't stop eating until both the Spam and a pack of crackers were gone. She forced herself to drink a full liter of bottled water, knowing she had to stay strong to stay sharp. She was puzzled by some feminine items in the bottom of the sack but thought it was better not to ask.

When Arnold turned off the television as soon as she finished her water she realized he had been watching her all along. He walked toward her, and she felt strong enough to fight him if that was what she had to do.

"I'd let you have the lounge chair, but I've got a slipped disk in my lower back," Arnold said. He handed her some scratchy wool blankets and went back to his side of the warehouse.

Gale arranged the blankets and tried to understand the apparent benevolence of her kidnapper. For some reason it seemed he was putting himself in danger in order to help her. He scared her, but his partner terrified her. Like every other woman and girl on the planet she had felt unwanted stares and uncomfortable glances before, but Blondie was different. The way he looked at her, leering at her and enjoying her discomfort, chilled her soul.

Soon Arnold was snoring heavily and Gale heard mice and rats scampering across the floor. She clutched the sharp lid in her hand and rolled herself into a tight cocoon with the blankets. She did not want to be bothered by mice or any other vermin while she tried to sleep.

Chapter Seven

The small creek that Hall's GPS led him to had no name and was not much different than the hundreds of others that fed and drained Port Royal Sound. From here he could see the tops of some of the fine old houses on The Bluff and the hospital beyond. The mouth of the creek was only about forty yards wide, but the oyster beds and tide lines indicated that it was nearly twice that width at high tide. Hall slowed and began to monitor his depth finder more closely. The display showed that the water was eight feet deep right now, but he knew a sand-bar or oyster rake could jump up from the bottom and snag his propeller with little warning.

Jimmy Barnwell impressed Hall the first day they were on the water together by never even turning the depth finder on. He told Hall it had taken him years to learn the waters that well and every once in a while a storm would come through and force him to learn everything all over again, occasionally at the expense of a new prop.

Even though he was worried about running aground, Hall couldn't help but notice the beauty of his surroundings. To his left, (port, Jimmy would have corrected) the marsh was uninterrupted for miles. It stretched from the creek to the firm soil of St. Helena Island, one of the few Sea Islands that had not completely fallen prey to developers' ambitions. Many of the island's residents were African Americans who were descended from freed slaves. People still farmed here. Tomatoes, corn, decorative flowers. The only surviving institution of the Port Royal Experiment, the Penn School, was less than five miles away from where he now floated.

The creek halved in size as he rounded a bend, and he saw an older woman and a young girl in a boat in the middle of the creek. They were in a beautiful, old but restored Chris Craft runabout Hall guessed had been built before the Second World War. He saw hundreds of dead fish floating in the creek water and a rainbow sheen danced on the wake from his boat.

Hall waved to the two ladies and took a notebook out of the waterproof compartment under his seat. Any type of fish kill had to be investigated and all fuel spills had to be reported to the Coast Guard. He asked the lady a few questions and made notes for several minutes, then snapped a few photographs before he started collecting evidence.

"Why are you wearing gloves?" a girl in the boat asked Hall. She looked to be the age of a middle-schooler.

"Just in case," Hall said. "Whatever killed these fish may not be healthy for me."

Hall collected six dead fish. Two striped mullet, one ladyfish, two immature redfish (spottail bass) and one pinfish. Each specimen was packaged individually in a ziplock bag. He recorded the location, date, and time of the collection on the outside of each bag and all of the samples went into a small cooler with some ice he had brought along just for this purpose. He would put them in his freezer when he got back home and tomorrow would pack them in dry ice and overnight them to the U.S. Fish and Wildlife Service forensics laboratory in Oregon. Within a week he should know what specific toxin had killed these fish.

"Thanks for calling this in," Hall told the lady.

"I'm glad to help. I hope you can catch who is responsible for this. We've all got to help if there is to be any beauty left for my grandchildren to enjoy. Please tell Gale that I said hello, Officer." For a few minutes he had enjoyed playing biologist.

Hall said he would relay the message to Gale and decided to stay in the creek while he recorded his observations. Hall grabbed the chain and slipped his anchor over the side and the engine on the old Chris Craft rumbled to life behind him. When he let go of the chain and watched the anchor disappear into the water he realized that he never re-tied the anchor to the line after trying to lasso the dolphin. He hoped the good citizens hadn't noticed his mistake, and knew he had to make a trip to the marine supply store.

After making his notes and giving Grandma a good head start Hall left the small creek at thirty—knots, cruising speed for his patrol boat. Clouds were building in the southwest sky and Hall wondered if the low-pressure system coming up from the Gulf of Mexico was a little ahead of schedule. Never in his life had he paid as much attention to the weather as he did now, since it was as important to him as the thermostat setting was for those poor souls that slaved away in cubicle farms. More important, he realized. Out here the weather could kill him. The paperwork he needed to complete gave him an excuse to head for home and he did so, adjusting his course across the sound so that he wasn't heading directly into the small whitecaps.

Pinckney showed her best side when he came in from the sound. A back barrier island, Pinckney did not have any ocean frontage. It was sheltered from the salt spray and strong winds by Hilton Head Island which lay across Skull Creek. The National Wildlife Refuge consumed all of Pinckney Island and a few thousand acres of tidal marsh. Tall sabal palmettos whose likeness graced the state flag towered over tropical saw palmettos. The loblolly pine trees grew as straight as rails and were like adolescents towering over their elder oaks and hickories. A working plantation for over one hundred years, the Fish and Wildlife Service was restoring the maritime forest and wetlands on the island to their natural state. Drainage ditches that had drained the swampy inland areas were being filled in and agricultural fields were allowed to turn fallow. In a few years it would appear as it would have been if man had never settled there, Hall thought.

When he got to the tip of the island he saw a small animal walking along the shoreline. It was the size of a small raccoon but wasn't acting like one. He took out his binoculars for a closer look and saw that it was a small dog. A puppy. He looked around for any human companions and didn't see any.

Dogs were not allowed in the refuge under any circumstances. A single dog could destroy dozens of shorebird nests looking for a single meal and the birds had a tough enough time with the raccoons and the snakes. Jimmy Barnwell told him the refuge was a popular spot to drop off unwanted cats and dogs.

The puppy was barking at the water and Hall was close enough to see that it looked like a black lab. He switched off the outboard engine and tilted it out of the water, letting the momentum carry the boat until it nudged the bottom and stopped several yards from the shore.

Hall whistled and called for the dog to come to him. The pup ignored him and kept barking, splashing now in the shallow water. Hall walked to the front of his boat and looked at the water. The sandy bottom looked firm enough so he slipped off his shoes and rolled up his pants legs. The water was cool and the sand slipped between his toes. He took two steps and sank to his knees in mud that was hidden beneath the sand.

The mud created a powerful suction and each step he took was an effort. After about fifteen steps he reached the firmer sand of the beach and walked toward the dog. To his surprise the puppy ran to him and bit him playfully on his thumb when he reached to pet it. Hall picked it up and realized too late that the black dog was covered with the same ooze he had just walked through, and now his khaki shirt was covered with odiferous muck from the marsh.

When he began to walk back to his boat the puppy started barking again and tried to jump out of his arms. Hall looked back over his shoulder and thought a log he had seen at the edge of the water was now moving toward him. Then he realized it was a large alligator following him and it was making much better progress through the mud. He looked at the distance between him and the gator and how much farther it was to the boat and knew it was going to be close.

By the time he was five feet from the boat the water was deep enough that the alligator was swimming, and was swimming much faster than Hall could walk. He threw the puppy into the boat and grabbed for the boat railing as the water exploded behind him. He felt the rough skin of the gator against his leg as he pulled himself onto the bow and plunged headfirst onto the deck.

On shaky legs he stood and peered into the water which was cloudy from the silt and sediment that had been stirred up. The alligator was nowhere to be seen. The puppy was standing quietly next to him and there was blood mixed with the mud that was covering the bottom of the boat.

After confirming he still had two feet and ten toes, Hall sat down and checked the bottom of his feet. A knife—sharp oyster shell was stuck in the instep of his left foot. There was a gallon jug of fresh water under the console and he used it to clean his wound and hoped that he wouldn't have to get any stitches. He wondered if the alligator knew it was one of the endangered species he was sworn to protect.

The puppy bounded out of the boat without any help when they reached the dock at the cottage. It scampered ahead of him and he limped behind, leaving alternate bloody and muddy footprints on the weathered wood. After hosing off his feet he turned the water on the puppy and sprayed all the mud off of him. When he reached down to pet him the pup nipped at his hand again.

"I think I'll call you Belker," he said.

Chapter Eight

For Hall McCormick the day started at four-thirty in the morning when Belker whined to go outside. Last night's thunderstorm had left everything smelling fresh and new, and while the dog took care of urgent business, Hall dressed and planned his day. He wanted to call Jimmy and ask him about the monthly reports, then pick up some lumber in the afternoon. The puppy followed him out onto the dock and jumped into the boat when he stepped aboard to start the engine. Belker barked at the dark water, and Hall looked to make sure no more logs were swimming toward his boat.

The boat engine idled down a few hundred RPM's when it was warm, and Hall took the puppy back to the cottage and locked him in the kitchen. He would need to take him to the vet if he planned on keeping him.

"Try not to get eaten today," he whispered.

There was just a hint of pink on the horizon as he ran with the tide out of Calibogue Sound and into the Atlantic Ocean. He and Jimmy had been right here less than twenty-four hours ago, but it felt like a week had gone by. The black-white-black pattern of the Tybee Island lighthouse came into view as he hugged the shoreline of Dafauskie Island and continued south. He was closer to the Savannah National Wildlife Refuge than he was to his home refuge, but the Savannah Refuge was over twenty-nine thousand acres so the refuge officer assigned to Pinckney Island worked the water. This agreement spread the workload between the officers in both refuges, although they both had the same boss and helped each other out on occasion.

Several shrimp trawlers were coming in from their night's work and Hall was going to check their catch. Last winter was mild and Hall knew the fishermen were hopeful for a good "roe" shrimp season. The spring season lasted only a month, and in a good year statewide harvests could exceed half a million pounds. Hall was required to make a certain number of commercial boardings every month to ensure the fishermen were adhering to federal regulations. Unlike a dolphin rescue, it was something he had done before. He and Jimmy boarded enough shrimp boats while he was in training for Hall to realize there was no way for him to know how he would be received. They had been cursed by a captain who had no violations and apologized to by a skipper who received a citation.

Calibouge Lady had had a good night's fishing and the attitude of the crew reflected it. Hall secured his boat by the bow line and was helped aboard by a crewman, letting the trawler tow his patrol boat behind. He heard and felt the boat speed up once he was safely aboard.

"Show 'em the TED's, boys," the captain ordered.

The crew lowered the nets onto the deck so Hall could inspect and measure the Turtle Exclusion Devices, a small tunnel in the net that was supposed to let endangered sea turtles escape. Jimmy told Hall that the devices were loathed by the shrimpers who knew that valuable shrimp also escaped and that the turtles rarely survived after tumbling along through the net and out the "Ted."

The three men on the shrimp boat were black, as were most of the shrimpers that Hall and Jimmy stopped together. Sometimes their thick accents made them hard for Hall to understand. Other times, when they didn't want to be understood by outsiders, they spoke in Gullah-a beautiful, almost extinct language of many of the lowcountry natives. Many of the words they spoke were borrowed from African dialects, Caribbean islanders and Jamaican Creoles and represented the heritage of the speakers.

Jimmy schooled Hall not only in the lay of the land and the depth of the waters but in the history of the region as well. Hall felt sorry for many of the residents of Dafauskie Island and other coastal areas who had lived in blissful indifference to progress for generations until developers raped their homeland. Folks who never knew they were poor and underprivileged sold their invaluable sea islands for the chance at a better life and watched their children grow up, move away, and take the future with them. Most realized too late that happiness couldn't be bought, but it could be sold. Golf resorts and million dollar waterfront estates erased a century and a half of heritage in a few short years. Perhaps statutory rape was a better definition.

"Take some home for supper, Cap'n." The old sailor offered a plastic grocery sack full of large shrimp, so fresh they were still snapping and popping inside the bag.

Hall hesitated. He knew how important it was to gain the trust of the people, especially the fishermen. Ethics were just as important.

"Ain't done nothing wrong, so it can't be no graft," the wise old waterman reasoned.

Hall took the heavy bag of tasty shellfish and wished the crew luck on their next trip before he departed. He checked three more boats before eight a.m., citing one captain for a vessel with no fire extinguisher. All of the boats had Turtle Exclusion Devices on board, but when he was on the last boat a juvenile loggerhead turtle fell from the net when it was brought in. It thudded onto the deck with the shrimp and other bycatch-fish that would be thrown overboard, dead or alive. When one of the crewmen went to shovel the turtle up with what looked like a grain scoop, Hall stopped him.

He was wrong, it was not a loggerhead turtle. Hall flipped the dead reptile onto its stomach for a closer look. The head of the turtle was small and the carapace was a pale green, as if it were trying to mimic the green ocean it had been plucked from. The shells of loggerhead turtles were reddish-brown, almost coppery unless they were covered with barnacles and other epibionts. He lifted it and it was heavy. The size of a trashcan lid and thirty-five pounds, he guessed. Sad, lifeless eyes looked up at him.

"Ain't my fault," the shrimper said. Hall gave him a hard look.

Hall said "You didn't break any laws, but it would still be alive if you hadn't snagged it."

"Yeah, and who's gonna feed my kids?"

Hall quit the skirmish he could never win. He transferred the dead turtle to his boat and cast off.

Chapter Nine

He couldn't help but notice the girl was pretty, but Detective Carl Varnum knew that would soon fade. The girls who started out at the White Pony were young and attractive with clear eyes and a plan for the future. Most of them could have passed for one of his daughter's classmates in her senior year of high school. Within eight months to a year they would be at Sarge's or Twins, across the Jasper County line, better living through chemistry having taken its toll on their assets. Some would be prostitutes well before they were of legal drinking age.

Varnum had known a lot of strippers. The one sitting across from him in the booth at Waffle House was the latest one that owed him a favor. She was all blonde hair and silicone. Distracting. They were both smoking his cigarettes and she had ordered the All-Star Special with a side of hash browns since he was paying. She was drinking a Diet Coke with her breakfast, just like his daughter would have done. He waited for her to begin.

"I don't know if it means anything, but one of my customers said that he was getting ready to come into a big score."

She lost some of her beauty when she blew the cigarette smoke out of her nose. Varnum thought he noticed the beginning of tooth decay on one of her back teeth. Meth stripped the enamel off of teeth quicker than sugar ever could.

"Dope?" he asked.

"I don't think so. He buys from one of the guys at the club, so he must not have his own source. This is something else. Sometimes he meets another guy there, looks like he has money." She shoveled smothered and covered hash browns into her mouth with one hand and kept the lit cigarette in the other, taking puffs in between swallows.

"Name."

"Nuh-uh," she said with a mouthful of eggs. She swallowed and took another drag. "I got a license plate."

He wrote down the tag number she gave to him in his notebook and put it in his shirt pocket. He took a fifty from his wallet and put it on the table next to her plate.

Varnum asked "Why do you think he's not legit?"

"He's slimy," she said. Varnum didn't ask for specifics.

He handed her two business cards, his and one from a local church that had a ministry for girls in trouble.

"I don't need any help," she said. "I'm just doing this to get enough money to go back to nursing school. As soon as I get my boobs paid off I can start saving for college. Will you tell the judge I helped you?"

"Sure, if this turns into anything, I will. Not much to tell so far. Call me if you find out anything else. Better yet, call Reverend Phil. He can help you more than I ever could. What bank gave you a loan for a boob job?"

She had a mouthful of food and her cigarette had burned down to the filter. She gave him a look he was accustomed to with two children of his own.

"Bobby, the owner of the Pony. He loaned me the money. I'm paying them off while I dance at his place."

His unmarked patrol car was parked at the grocery store next door. When he walked over to it he ran his hand across the stubble of his crew cut, two days away from his weekly trip to the barber. The humidity was already making him feel sticky in his long sleeved dress shirt and neck tie. He remembered his first day as a detective when his wife told him that he could never, ever wear a tie with a short sleeved shirt unless he was selling appliances at Sears. She used to lay his clothes out for him the night before so he wouldn't wear anything that clashed.

He stood next to his car for a minute and finished his cigarette. A younger guy in a hooded sweatshirt came out of the restaurant and walked over to him.

"Anything worthwhile?" he asked. Varnum never met with a snitch alone. The plainclothes officer that was his close cover worked in narcotics.

"Who knows?" Varnum said. "She gave me a few tag numbers from some guy that has 'something big' going down. I probably wasted fifty bucks of the sheriff's money."

The younger cop shrugged. Every cop that ever had a snitch knew how the game was played.

"Later, Dude."

Varnum watched him go. His son called him "Dude". Once. Now he was in Iraq, choking on the same dust that his father had eaten twenty years ago. The empty nest wasn't all it was cracked up to be when there was no one to share it with.

When he was back in his cubicle he typed up a Contact Report and logged it into the system. He ran the tag numbers the girl had given him and then ran criminal histories on the owners. The first tag was assigned to an Audi, last year's model. The registered owner had no criminal history. He Googled the name and found out that he was a local real estate broker and developer. His web site claimed he had sold over ten million dollars in real estate every year for the past five years. Varnum did the math and decided this must be the guy who looked like he had money. His picture was superimposed over a drawing of his latest proposed development and Varnum printed it and started a new file.

The second tag belonged to a ten year old Trans Am registered to a woman who lived in Port Royal. A driver's license check under the same name and address indicated that the owner was a seventy year old woman. Mom. He ran the address through the state arrestee database and found that a subject that had just been released on parole listed that address as his home. He'd been released four months ago after serving a stretch for aggravated assault, forgery, and sexual assault. He seemed to be an interesting companion for a respected real estate developer. Varnum put the printouts of the parolee in the file with the other information.

Before he logged off he looked around to make sure that no one else was nearby and went to another website where he entered his user name and password. Hearts and hokey music greeted him but not a single private message. Twenty-three views, but no messages. There were two more days left in his month-long trial membership, but at this rate he didn't think he wanted to pay for the rejection he was getting for free.

The phone on his desk rang, and he made the mistake of answering it. One of his victims was on the phone, complaining that her son had run away again. He pulled up an old report on the computer and changed the date of occurrence, saving himself the trouble of starting from scratch.

Chapter Ten

" Can you assist us with a search and rescue mission?" Hall acknowledged the Coast Guard radio operator and switched the VHF base station in his kitchen to a channel that was restricted to use by emergency service agencies.

"We need you to search the area north and west of 32 degrees, 16'31.75 North and 80 degrees, 39'03.19 West. We are looking for a missing boat and boater. The boat is a twenty-two foot center console with a white hull and pictures of dolphins and sea turtles painted on it. The operator is a white female, twenty-six-years old. Missing since yesterday afternoon. Report back when you arrive in your search area and monitor this frequency for further information."

He acknowledged the request and confirmed the area he was assigned to search. Gale was missing? He couldn't believe someone hadn't called him earlier. He was supposed to take her to Jimmy's retirement party tonight. He guessed she'd gotten stuck on an oyster bar or had mechanical trouble. She was an old salt compared to him, and he knew he'd tease her about spending the night in her boat when he saw her this evening.

He'd gotten into the habit of starting his work day the same way that Jimmy used to, listening to the marine radio in the kitchen while he ate breakfast and checked the weather reports. He was not expecting the call from the Coast Guard this morning. His route to his search area would take him past Low Country Seafood, and he decided to stop there on the way. The first thing Hall noticed was that none of the shrimp boats were tied to the pier, which was unusual for this time of the day. The second thing he noticed was the Native Son sitting at the dock.

After tying his boat to the dock he went inside and saw the bearded dolphin rescuer hunched over a chart with an older man who Hall knew to be Gale's father. Both men looked up when he walked in.

"Can you help with the search?" Silas Pickens asked Hall.

"The Coast Guard wants me to check Cowen Creek and the marsh behind Distant Island."

"Alright," Silas said. "I'll check Capers Creek towards Frogmore. Maybe the storm blew her up on an oyster bed in there."

"I'll listen up on the radio," the older man said to them.

"By the way, I'm Gale's brother." Hall learned that Silas was the one who reported Gale missing.

"I didn't have a charter this morning, but I came in early to catch some bait for this afternoon. It isn't unusual for Gale to be out early, but I saw the lights on in her office and came in to say hello. She wasn't in her apartment upstairs, and I'm pretty sure she never came back last night."

"Do you know where she went yesterday? Hall asked.

"No. She usually stays inshore, but the outgoing tide was late afternoon yesterday and the thunderstorm came from the west. Either one could have blown her out to sea if the boat was disabled."

The older man answered a shrimper who was on the radio, reporting that he had not located anything yet. He had a cup full of steaming coffee in one hand and a mind full of concern.

Silas said, "We'll find her Pop. Don't worry."

Hall started his patrol boat, and Silas pushed his skiff away from the dock and drifted next to him.

"Dad's got his boats checking the ocean side of the islands with the Coasties."

"Are all of the shrimp boats out looking?" Hall asked. He thought that Low Country Seafood owned close to a dozen boats.

"Yeah. I'm going upriver. There's a couple of developments Gale was keeping an eye on up there. If she ran hard aground she'd be up there, maybe even out of radio contact."

The chances of Gale's boat being stuck and her radio and cell phone not working were pretty slim, Hall guessed. He hoped the ocean that she loved and worked so hard to protect returned her affection. By the time Hall was under way in his own boat, Silas and the Native Son were a small speck on the water speeding across Port Royal sound. Hall checked his chart and found the area he was supposed to search. He prayed he didn't find a body.

Chapter Eleven

H all slowed to avoid the wake of a rusty old barge as he crossed the sound. It was riding high in the water, telling Hall that it was empty. He waved to the captain and the captain waved back.

Easing the throttle back to idle speed, he nosed his patrol boat into Cowen Creek. It had taken Hall a while to realize that these "creeks", as they were called, were not the same type of creek he had grown up around in the piedmont of South Carolina. These bodies of water were tidal creeks, small fingers of water that filled with the rising tide and emptied with the ebb. Some were completely dry at low tide, while others were deep enough for a shrimp trawler at all stages of the tidal cycle. They created islands and inlets and brought life into the salt marsh. No two were the same and only the larger creeks or the ones where something significant happened had a name. Hall briefly wondered what or who Cowen Creek was named for.

A dolphin surfaced next to his boat and exhaled loudly, startling him. The large mammal paced him for several hundred yards until she disappeared underneath the water. Far ahead Hall saw another dolphin, or perhaps the same one, chasing a school of fish. With his binoculars, Hall saw two dolphins and they were working together, herding mullet against the muddy shoreline. The dolphins swam into the tightly packed school of baitfish and chased them onto on the muddy shore coming almost completely out of the water. Hall thought that one of the dolphins had a scar near its blowhole and wondered if this was the dolphin he met yesterday. He watched them work for a while, impressed with their predatory skills. The water was too muddy for them to be able to see the mullet they were feeding on, and Hall knew they were using echolocation to track their prey and it was more precise than any man made sonar could ever hope to be. They moved with grace and precision and caught more fish in a few minutes than Hall caught in a year.

The creek twisted and turned but maintained a broad width and good depth. He rounded a bend and caught sight of a boat and his heart beat faster, but only for a second. The two fishermen he spoke with had not heard about the missing boat but promised to keep an eye out for it. Hall continued back into the marsh, reasoning that Gale could have been at the terminus of the creek before the fishermen arrived.

The end of Cowen Creek came into view, and Hall radioed his report to the Coast Guard. He checked the other creeks in his search area, and in the late afternoon he called the Coast Guard to see if there was somewhere else they wanted him to search. After he received his new instructions, someone else called him on the radio.

"Hall, pick me up at the marina." It was Jimmy Barnwell.

Thankfully, Hall was able to pull into an empty boat slip next to Jimmy's pristine sailboat. Jimmy hopped aboard in civilian clothes, and they left the marina before he spoke. Hall noticed he had his pistol in a holster underneath his life jacket.

"I didn't hear about Gale until this afternoon. Rebecca and I had to pick up a few more things for dinner tonight." Jimmy finally said.

Hall only nodded. They were in one of the smaller creeks near Parris Island when they heard the bad news on the radio.

A Coast Guard helicopter crew found Gale's boat adrift, seven miles offshore from Fripp Inlet. The helicopter crew didn't see anyone aboard, but a state wildlife officer was close by and was en-route to recover the boat. Both Jimmy and Hall knew that Gale's boat didn't have a cabin. If she were on board, they would have seen her from the air. They rode back to the Beaufort Municipal Marina in silence.

"Hell of a way to start retirement," Jimmy said when he stepped out of his old patrol boat. Rebecca was surprised to see them back so soon and knew without asking. Hall wondered how many times this scene had been repeated during Jimmy's career.

Hall felt compelled to do more but didn't know what he could do. As much as he wanted to help, his boat wasn't designed to take on the open ocean. The state wildlife agency and the Coast Guard were responsible for investigating boating accidents and for continuing the search for the body. Hall hated even to think it, but the water temperature was in the low sixties, and it didn't take hypothermia long to overpower the hardiest of souls. He feared he'd lost a friend and that possibly something more precious had been lost. He couldn't go home if there was a chance she was still out there, alive and in need of help. He filled the tank on his patrol boat at the marina and headed back out into the sound.

Most of the shrimp boats had returned to Low Country Seafood when he passed by after midnight on his way home. After securing his boat at his dock, he took the shrimp out of his cooler and carried it inside. A newcomer to the coast, shrimp were still an extravagance to him, but he couldn't bring himself to eat. Would he ever see Gale again? Belker seemed to sense his mood and was content to quietly follow him around the house.

He'd forgotten about the turtle until he heard Belker barking and went outside to investigate. Hall found a guidebook on a shelf in the den, and in a few minutes he'd identified it as an olive ridley turtle, not rare but still listed as an endangered species. He'd never cleaned a turtle before, and after an hour he looked like he'd been on the losing end of a knife fight. He dumped the meat and entrails into the water, put the shell on top of an ant hill in his back yard and looked at his watch. After eighteen hours Uncle Sam had gotten his money's worth. Soon he and Belker were snoring together on the couch.

Chapter Twelve

G ale woke in a panic, unable to remember where she was and why she was there, and her panic did not subside when she remembered. She rolled out of her cocoon, and looked over at Arnold who was lying motionless on the chaise lounge chair. There was just enough light spilling through the lone window for her to see everything in her cell. Her bladder was so full it hurt, but she wasn't sure what to do about it.

She said, "I have to use the bathroom."

The lumpy form under the covers did not move.

"I need to use the BATHROOM!"

Arnold kicked his legs until he was free of his blanket and sat on the edge of his makeshift bed with his head in his hands. Then he walked over toward her, and Gale pulled the blanket tight around her shoulders, but Arnold walked right past her and stopped at a piece of plywood that was lying on the floor. He gripped the edge and pulled it up, revealing a jagged hole, walked back to his side of the room and returned with a roll of toilet paper. He handed it to her, went back to his lounge chair and covered himself with the blanket.

The handcuff on her ankle had rubbed her raw, and the rusty chain clanked as she walked across the floor. Her toilet was a hole in the floor, about eighteen inches across. The marsh mud was visible though the opening. Low tide. She thought she could squeeze through the hole if she ever got free from the chain. She waited until she was certain that Arnold had gone back to sleep before she squatted and hovered over the hole.

The horrible odor she smelled was her own body. She stunk from getting sick on herself, from the tainted mud in the barge, from fear. Maybe smelling like a horse rode hard and put up wet was a good thing in her current situation. She couldn't bathe, check her email, or brush her teeth, but she was able to perform one of her morning rituals. She started with Downward Facing Dog stretches and finished her yoga session thirty minutes later in the Warrior position feeling physically and mentally refreshed from her workout.

An hour after she finished her exercises Arnold rose again, and walked out the door. Gale heard him pee off of the dock into the water, then he came back inside. He opened a soda and a box of Pop Tarts and tossed her one of the packages. She avoided junk food under normal circumstances, but she knew that she had to eat. She washed them down with a bottle of water and brushed her teeth with one of the few clean spots on her shirt. Arnold turned on the small black and white television.

He was soon riveted to a talk show featuring a woman who was waiting on a paternity test to see which of her cousins was the father of her unborn child. Members of the studio audience egged on the participants, and two of the possible fathers got into a fist fight and had to be restrained. During a commercial break a news update flashed on the screen, and she saw an aerial view of her boat being towed in from the ocean. Snow white with a mural of fish and turtles painted on the hull, there wasn't another boat like it on the east coast. A Coast Guard officer was talking about hypothermia and how quickly someone would succumb to the elements, even in mild weather. The commentator said the search for the missing boater had been suspended and a picture of her, from the press packet that was distributed when she became Soundkeeper, flashed across the screen. She recognized several of her Coastwatchers who were keeping vigil at a local church.

After the news broadcast ended the station returned to the train wreck already in progress. Gale turned away from the television, and bit the inside of her cheek so she wouldn't cry. She did not want to show any weakness or vulnerability, but she was terrified. She knew that there could only be one reason why Arnold was keeping her, and it made her sick to her stomach. She had to control her breathing to keep from hyperventilating.

Her boat had been found adrift at sea, and the search had been called off. No one was looking for her anymore.

The topless bar opened at noon, and Blondie was the first customer. Like most patrons of the White Pony he mistakenly believed that one of the dancers fancied him, believing her feelings had nothing to do with the fact that he stuffed a twenty in her g-string each time she danced for him. Blondie knew it made the man he was doing business with nervous to meet him here—another reason he liked the place.

Thirty minutes and three drinks later his other partner arrived. Just as he had done every time before, he sat at the bar and looked all around the dimly lit room. When he seemed satisfied, he joined Blondie at his table.

"Buy me a drink." Blondie ordered.

The man hailed a waitress and gave her a twenty for the ten dollar drink. Then he looked all around the bar again.

"Relax," Blondie said. "It's not like you've got a truckload of coke sitting outside."

This off-hand remark only made the real estate developer more nervous, regretting the day he'd ever met his accomplice.

Mark Lancaster had bought a fifteen parcel lot outside of Beaufort with plans to cram three hundred condominiums on it and run with the profits to Florida, Mecca of shady land deals. Two days after he closed on the land his dream ended abruptly. The land, for which he had mortgaged everything he owned, failed to pass environmental standards for development. The soil was contaminated and possibly the groundwater.

After a day of research at the Registrar of Deeds, which should have been done before the purchase, Lancaster learned a sawmill had occupied the land thirty years ago. It supplied wooden ties for the railroad and had huge tanks of creosote that the railroad ties were dipped in. After that process the railroad ties cured and aged in the sun. Just like a telephone pole sweating in the summer sun, the railroad ties bled chemicals into the earth for decades. The warehouse that replaced the sawmill when it closed wasn't required to submit to the stricter residential environmental standards since it was zoned as an industrial site. When Mark Lancaster petitioned for a zoning variance, the soil and water had to be tested and his world came crashing down around him.

Sitting in his construction trailer one night, crying in his wine over an artist's renditions of his condos, he heard a noise outside. Peering into the darkness he saw two men wrestle a heavy box out of the trunk of a car and begin to beat on it with something. Emboldened by more than a few glasses of Chardonnay, he grabbed his pistol and a flashlight and met Arnold and Blondie who were trying to break into a safe. As drunk and despondent people often do, Mark Lancaster soon poured out his troubles to the two strangers. Soon a proposal was offered and accepted.

The State of South Carolina was responsible for testing the soil, and Beaufort County was responsible for certifying that the groundwater was free from contamination. Mark Lancaster had bribed the county inspector during the development of two other properties. One phone call and a twenty-thousand dollar payment cleared that hurdle once again.

But the state inspector was a prick with principles and couldn't be bribed. A company approved by the EPA wanted over two-hundred thousand dollars to remove and properly dispose of the tainted earth, more than Mark Lancaster could afford. Arnold and Blondie promised to get rid of the dirt for fifty grand, and the deal was struck.

The envelope Mark Lancaster handed to Blondie contained ten-thousand dollars and the key to a dump truck that was sitting outside. Mark Lancaster would drive Blondie's car back to his hotel while Blondie did whatever he did with the load of bad dirt. Mark Lancaster didn't care.

"It's going to cost a little more than I figured," Blondie said as he took the money.

"What do you mean?" he whispered. "We had a deal."

"Maybe you want to get an estimate from someone else to finish the job? I've removed ten truck loads so far and it looks like it will take ten more to get it all out of there."

Blondie gave Mark a look that chilled him to the bone. Mark had seen his violent streak once before when he pulled a switchblade on Arnold and threatened to cut his balls off for flirting with his favorite dancer. Ever since then Blondie came to their meetings alone.

"Day after tomorrow, same time. Bring another ten grand."

Mark Lancaster started to protest but realized it wouldn't do him much good. A girl with big boobs and lots of curly blonde hair climbed on top of their table and started grinding her hips to the heavy metal music blaring from the speakers. Blondie took a hundred dollar bill from the envelope and stuffed it into her g-string until it disappeared. Mark Lancaster left the bar, drove Blondie's old Trans Am to the motel, and caught a taxi home.

Chapter Thirteen

He was suffocating. Each breath became harder and harder until the struggle to breathe woke him fully. Through half opened eyes Hall realized Belker was sitting on his chest and staring at him. He hoped the puppy could control his bladder for a few more seconds.

The pup scampered outside and disappeared behind a tangle of marsh elders. Hall walked out on the weathered wooden dock and checked the lines that secured his boat. The tide could rise and fall over ten feet in a thirteen hour period, and it took a good deal of thought to secure a boat properly. The challenge was to tie the boat loosely enough that the rising water didn't swamp the boat and the falling water didn't leave it suspended above the water.

The boat was fine, and when he gazed out over the water he thought about Gale Pickens. He knew she was an outstanding sailor and these were her waters. The small thunderstorm the previous night shouldn't have challenged her or her boat, but Hall knew the sea could be unforgiving. All it took was a misplaced step on a slippery deck or a rogue wave. A distracted moment could spell disaster.

Hall tried to reach a suitable conclusion and remembered something from his training, a phrase he believed in the first time he heard it.

"If something doesn't look right, find out why."

Criminal Investigation, to his surprise, was his favorite course in the law enforcement training. The instructor was a retired sheriff from Georgia who thrilled them with stories about moonshiners and bloody family squabbles. Renowned for his interrogation techniques, he was also a frequent guest lecturer at the FBI training academy in Quantico. The old sheriff was Columbo and Andy Griffith woven together with peach flavored chewing tobacco. Hall found the procedures used to solve a crime weren't all that different from the scientific process he used in the laboratory.

What didn't look right about Gale's disappearance? He needed more information before he could answer that question. He needed to talk to Silas Pickens and his father and find out who had seen Gale last, and where. Hall wrote down a few questions in the notebook he kept in his boat and called for Belker before going inside.

Just before he fell asleep again Hall remembered he hadn't closed and locked the gate to the parking area on the other end of the island. The gate was supposed to be locked at sundown, and the refuge maintenance staff was off for the Memorial Day weekend. Hall had agreed to lock the gate to the parking lot while they were gone. He went outside and started his other government issued vehicle, a navy-blue pick up truck.

Belker was too small to see over the dashboard, so he rode on Hall's lap to get a better view. The driveway that led from the highway to the caretaker's cottage was the main road on the island and was only a sand track covered with pine needles. Only official vehicles were allowed past the parking lot. Hall's truck, tractors, and the biologists SUV's were the only motorized vehicles that ever used the roads, but they were popular with visitors who used them for hiking or bicycle riding.

Hall drove through the tunnel of spooky Spanish moss hanging from low tree limbs. Soon the forest surrendered to open marsh, and the road was only a few inches above sea level. Hall could see for miles in every direction.

When he pulled into the parking lot his headlights played across a small sports car parked in the far end of the gravel lot, next to the trash dumpster. The windows were fogged over, and he waited a moment for the occupants to realize that they were no longer alone. When no one stirred he pulled closer and got out with his flashlight.

As soon as he climbed out of his truck Hall heard a girl's voice coming from the car. It was apparent from the pitch of her voice that her "no" wasn't being heeded. Hall snatched open the driver's door and shined his flashlight inside.

The girl screamed and the young man cursed when the beam from the flashlight blinded him. He was on top of her in the passenger seat, and she had tears streaming down her face. Hall grabbed him by the collar of his shirt and yanked him out of the car. Stinking of liquor, the young man bowed up and tried to pull away.

"Knock it off. I'm a police officer," Hall said. "Refuge Enforcement Officer" took too long to get out. "What's going on here?" Belker was at their feet, barking and snapping at the boy's ankles.

The young man, whose driver's license showed him to be nineteen years old, did all of the talking. He and his date were just trying to talk, he insisted. The girl stayed quiet until Hall talked to her away from her companion. Hall learned the boy who had been assaulting her was only an acquaintance who had offered her a ride home. She was only fifteen. Hall frisked him for weapons and turned his attention back to the girl.

When he glanced back at the boy he had returned to his car and was rummaging underneath his seat probably trying to ditch the alcohol since he shouldn't have had it in the car. He grabbed the boy's wrist and pulled him back out of the car. Then he radioed for someone to transport the kid to jail. It was against the law to possess alcohol in the wildlife refuge, and he committed an assault in Hall's presence. He needed to experience being locked up.

A young deputy sheriff arrived, and Hall gave him the details of what had occurred. While Hall filled out the arrest paperwork for illegal possession of alcohol the deputy searched the sports car. What he found under the driver's seat gave Hall a chill in spite of the muggy weather.

"Looks like you can add carrying a concealed weapon to that ticket, Warden."

Hall didn't bother to tell the deputy that he wasn't a game warden. It was a common error. Most law enforcement officers did not know that there were over 300 federal refuge enforcement officers across the country. He looked up from the paperwork, and saw the pistol that had been concealed under the driver's seat of the sports car. Hall realized for the first time that his duty pistol and other equipment were back at the cottage. He had only intended to lock up the parking lot and didn't think he would need it.

Now he had a decision to make. Carrying a concealed weapon on the refuge was a violation of federal law as well as the South Carolina Criminal Code. Through a formal Memorandum of Understanding between the U.S. Fish and Wildlife Service and the State of South Carolina, Hall had concurrent jurisdiction. In his position as a federal refuge enforcement officer he had the authority to enforce federal laws on or off of property owned by the U.S. Government. The MOU authorized Hall to act upon any violation of state law he encountered in the course of his official duties.

He had two citation books, one for violations of federal misdemeanors, which required the offender to appear before the federal magistrate in Beaufort. The other was a state ticket book, the same one used by deputies, police officers, and highway patrolmen throughout South Carolina. The young man was going to jail for carrying a concealed weapon, that much was certain. If Hall decided to charge him in the federal system he would have to go to the county jail with the deputy, wake up the on-duty U.S. Marshal in Columbia and submit a Statement of Probable Cause to the Assistant U.S. Attorney within twenty-four hours. In all the weeks that he had trained with Jimmy they'd never charged anyone with a federal crime, preferring instead the ease of the state system of criminal justice. Hall stuck with what he knew.

While the deputy began his paperwork Hall had a chance to think about what had happened. It scared him to think that the boy could have been reaching for a gun instead of a liquor bottle, as he had supposed. He didn't want to think about what could have happened to the girl if he hadn't forgotten to lock the gate. He didn't want to think about what would have happened if the kid would have shot him, either. Life was safer in a lab. Tomorrow he would lock up the gate earlier and he wouldn't forget his gun and equipment. He had been taught to handcuff first and search later. He vowed not to make that mistake again. His frustration grew again when the deputy returned.

"No assault case. She won't press charges," he told Hall.

The prisoner in the back of the deputy's car smiled when he heard this, and Hall knew everything was screwed up. Why did the guy going to jail have a smile on his face, and the cop who'd arrested him feel like he'd already lost the case?

Chapter Fourteen

No matter how bad the previous day had been a new dawn usually helped Hall put things in perspective. But the horizon dawned gray and over-cast, and the death of a friend was not forgotten overnight. He already wore the heavy and cumbersome gunbelt when he walked with Belker down the sandy driveway.

Before he had walked a quarter of a mile he could see Mackay Creek where it met the Chechessee River. The water in Mackay Creek flowed both ways; Northeast with the rising tide and Southwest when the water drained back toward the Atlan-tic. The wind blew in Hall's face, and he saw whitecaps on the water. His home was sheltered from this wind by the island itself, and he decided to use the weather as an excuse to stay off of the water for a day. He had plenty of work to do on dry ground, he reasoned, and the rough water would make it too dangerous to make any boardings or stop any boaters.

After their walk, master and man's best friend went to a pile of lumber stacked neatly behind the cottage. There were nine sheets of three-quarter inch plywood, one to cover every door and window of the small house during violent storms. There were also a dozen salt cured poles that appeared to be miniature telephone pole. The poles were twelve inches around at the base and tapered to six inches, twenty feet later. They weighed almost one-hundred pounds each. Hall selected one of them, and set to work after he took off his pistol belt and laid it on the seat of his truck.

He put the heavy pole on top of two sawhorses and retrieved a ragged set of plans from the tool shed. Jimmy's sharp handwriting and drawings detailed how to build an osprey nesting platform. This wasn't a specific task for him as a refuge officer but it was something he wanted to do. Jimmy taught him that while law enforcement was his primary responsibility, he was expected to help out with other tasks that needed to be completed in the refuge. Jimmy had taken on the responsibility of building the platforms years ago and Hall planned to keep the tradition alive.

As a wildlife refuge Pinckney Island was not just a nature preserve, but was actively managed for the benefit of all natural things, both plant and animal. Avian life was particularly abundant. Egrets, red knots, royal terns and endangered wood storks abounded. The grand American bald eagle was a common visitor to the refuge and hopefully a future resident.

The ospreys, or "fish hawks", as the locals called them, were already year-round residents of Pinckney Island. There were two nesting pair of osprey on the island that had been documented by members of the local Audubon Society last year on the annual Christmas Day bird count. Found on every continent except Antarctica near lakes, rivers, and the coast, osprey were magnificent to watch when they plucked fish from the water. Hall had seen osprey all of his life, on camping and fishing trips and in Charleston when he was in college. Their distinct arched wings in flight made them easy to identify, and it seemed to him the large birds of prey were much better at catching fish than he was. He remembered from his studies osprey were the only raptor that could grab an object with two toes in the front and two toes behind, giving it a very strong grip and they could close their nostrils to keep water out when they dove feet-first onto their prey.

Of the two pair of ospreys that called Pinckney Island home, only one pair nested in a tree. The other pair built their nest on a tall platform that had been erected just for that purpose. Hall was building another. The nest of an osprey could weigh several hundred pounds, so the plans called for stout timbers and solid construction.

The time passed quickly as he worked and soon the platform was finished and he bolted it to the pole. He ate a sandwich on the dock in front of his house and watched the male fiddler crabs wave their grossly disproportional claws at the wind, trying to attract a mate. Hall wasn't their type but waved back anyway. They didn't seem to notice. When he was finished eating, he strapped the platform in the bed of his truck and sat Belker in his lap.

He dragged the platform and pole as close as he could to the spot that he and Jimmy had selected for the new platform. This platform would overlook Buzzard Island, a small collection of oyster shells and marsh grass that all but disappeared on the highest tides. This site had been selected because it was far enough away from the other nests and it was accessible by vehicle.

The post hole diggers he used were the long-handled type used by utility workers. The soft sand yielded easily to his efforts, and soon the hole was thirty-six inches deep. The nesting platform was now fifteen feet above him and as he packed the last of the sand around the base of the post, Belker started barking at the nearby water. A splash and a large flock of gulls and terns caught his eye.

At first Hall thought a few dolphins were menacing a school of fish, but he saw that this was not the case. Below the circling and raucous birds were several dolphins, perhaps a dozen in all. They were packed together tightly as they slowly swam with the falling tide toward Port Royal Sound. Hall retrieved a pair of binoculars from his truck for a closer look and was astonished by what he saw.

The dolphins were swimming so closely together that they formed a floating raft. On top of their bodies, fully out of the water, they carried a single dolphin. Hall never saw the passenger dolphin move, and after watching for a while was pretty sure it was dead. One of the dolphins near the front of the group had a few fresh wounds around its nose, and Hall wondered if it had been the one that had been entangled in the net. He watched the curious procession until the mammals were out of sight.

Belker had quieted with the strange passing, and Hall sat on the tailgate of his truck. He was not sure of what he had just witnessed, but hoped the small library of nature guides and reference books at the cottage would give him a clue. By the time he collected his tools and drove back to his house it was late afternoon. One of the features he liked the best about his cottage was the outdoor shower attached to the back of the house and open except for a partition of faded wood that hid everything between his knees and shoulders. The beach houses his family had rented throughout the summers of his youth all had outdoor showers, he remembered. He had a great view of the sound when he showered but was able to maintain his modesty in case any boaters ventured too close.

He emptied his pockets, kicked off his boots and stepped into the shower with his clothes on. He considered this a pre-wash for his muddy and sweaty clothes. After they were soaked he stripped and scrubbed, turning the water to its hottest setting, which chased Belker away from his feet. As soon as he turned off the water he heard his cell phone beeping.

He recognized the missed call as the phone number for the Beaufort County Communications Center. The sheriff's department, volunteer fire departments, emergency management, and several other agencies used this central radio dispatching center. The woman who answered his call promptly put him on hold.

"Jimmy?" a man came on the line and asked him.

"No, this is Hall McCormick. Jimmy retired yesterday."

"I knew he was getting close, good for him. This is Sergeant Crickson in the communications center. We just received an anonymous tip that two men are going to be netting illegally in Euhaw Creek this evening."

Hall wrote the unfamiliar name on the palm of his damp hand.

"Can you respond? The state wildlife officer for our district isn't working today. He put in about twenty-four hours straight searching for the missing boater. We were hoping that you'd check out the report."

Hall assured the sergeant he would and disconnected. Poor planning, he thought as he padded through the kitchen with wet feet, looking for a towel. He threw his wet uniform in the washing machine that lived on the back porch and took a fresh pair of brown pants and a khaki shirt out of his closet. The Kevlar vest took as much getting used to as the heavy gunbelt did, but he strapped it on even though it was still damp and sweaty from wearing it yesterday, and pulled his shirt over it. His name and the badge of his office were embroidered on the front, and he thought that he looked trim and fit when he checked himself in the mirror.

"Sorry boy, not tonight," Hall told Belker. He left his puppy in the kitchen and went outside to his patrol boat. Threading through the channel markers that delineated the deep water from the shallow, a dolphin breached the surface of the water off of his starboard rail and blasted air out of its blowhole. Hall tooted the boat's horn in return.

Turning north after he cleared the lee of Pinckney Island, Hall crossed the headwaters of Port Royal Sound where the Chechessee and Broad Rivers met and headed inshore, northeast, on the Broad River. He took the chop head on, and the boat bounced hard over the water. He finally trimmed down the bow, which helped, but the salty spray still stung his eyes and ran off of his slicker.

It took him twenty minutes to reach the highway bridge, which he "dead-reckoned" to be the halfway point. It took him another half hour to find the mouth of Euhaw Creek after two short detours around some low water. He turned the boat motor off and considered his options.

According to his chart Euhaw Creek was less than two miles long. Hazzard Creek branched off of it and returned to the Broad River, but that small creek did not appear to be navigable. The wind and the tide were at odds with one another, and as a result Hall's boat stood still. He had seen only one boat, a tug, on his wet and windy trip. He decided to wait for any boat that headed for the creek and stop it for a routine inspection of safety equipment. Any illegal gill nets would be easy to find. The shadowy crescent of an early rising moon climbed above the palmettos on the horizon, and Hall appreciated the similarity to the flag of the state of South Carolina.

The VHF radio kept him company. First he listened to the marine forecast and then some shrimpers who were headed out to drag their nets overnight. One of them asked if Gale's body had been found yet, and someone answered that she was still missing. Hall scanned the water at all points of the compass with his binoculars and waited, just as cops had been doing since the beginning of time.

Two hours later he heard the sound of a boat engine. The sound carried on the wind, and he was unable to tell which direction it was coming from. Again he was reminded how far sound carried across water. He started his boat and eased out into the river and heard the engine on the other boat rev loudly. Then he realized it was in the creek behind him.

He turned his boat sideways and switched on his blue strobe light at the same time. The boat, a small jon boat that had camouflaged paint veered around him, and its propeller screamed as it struggled to get a bite of the water. The two men in the boat had seen him and didn't want to stop and chat.

Hall picked up his radio microphone to call for assistance when he remembered that no one else was available. He knew he was on his own, and for the first time the heavy weight on his hip felt reassuring.

The patrol boat was much faster than the small jon boat and Hall was soon within twenty yards of the fleeing suspects. He didn't want to get much closer because he knew they would soon run out of water at the end of the creek and would be forced to jump out of the boat or turn toward him. Hall decided he would not give way to the smaller craft. He would block the creek with his boat if they turned back toward him.

The passenger in the fleeing vessel busied himself with something in the bow of the boat, and Hall realized he was jettisoning the illegal nets. Hall slowed to go around the nets which would have fouled his propeller and ended the chase. When he cleared the obstruction he jammed the throttle as far forward as it would go and closed to within twenty feet of the boat. Neither man turned to look at him now, afraid of being identified later if they managed to escape.

Euhaw Creek twisted and turned and suddenly narrowed. Hall increased his following distance. A large white cooler flew out of the boat in front of him and glanced off the front of Hall's boat with a dull thud. The suspect's boat began to slow. Hall used his PA speaker, and ordered the men to raise their hands. They did as they had been instructed, and Hall drew his pistol and started to pull alongside.

Just as Hall was close enough to see that the boat had no registration numbers, it took off again. Hall holstered his pistol, cursed, and slammed the throttle forward all at once. The boat in front of him made a hard right turn into a narrow break in the marsh grass. Hazzard Creek, Hall correctly guessed. He knew he couldn't follow them when the wake from their small boat turned gray with mud. Hazzard Creek was too shallow for his boat. Both men flipped him the bird just before they disappeared in the marsh grass.

Hall turned off his strobe light and slowly motored out of Euhaw Creek. The white cooler was almost submerged when he found it, and he struggled to get it on his boat. It was full of juvenile redfish, illegal to possess even if they had been caught legally with a rod and reel. To keep the abandoned net from becoming a hazard to navigation he hauled it on board too. It was good evidence, but he had no one to use it against.

Running now with both the tide and the wind, Hall made the trip back down the river in just less than thirty minutes. The ride was much smoother and drier, but instead of taking the familiar route home he turned into the Beaufort River.

The Penn School on St. Helena Island was founded by Pennsylvania abolitionists in 1862, before the Emancipation Proclamation was signed by President Abraham Lincoln. Its purpose was to educate the freed slaves on the sea islands of Port Royal Sound and did so for many generations. Dr. Martin Luther King Jr. held his annual Southern Christian Leadership Conference on the Penn campus for several years, and it was named a national National Historic Landmark by the Department of the Interior in 1974.

Hall knew none of this when he pulled up to the rickety dock that protruded into Cowen Creek behind the Penn Center. He only knew Jimmy had told him that any fish he confiscated were to be delivered to this place.

An old man who reminded Hall of the shrimpers he had met helped him carry the cooler into the kitchen of the small school. The cook and headmistress thanked him profusely for the fish and his generosity. He apologized for not letting them keep the cooler, but made up for it by staying and helping clean the catch.

"You've cleaned a lot of fish," the old man said after a while. Hall's pistol belt and uniform shirt were hanging on a chair behind them. It was the first time the old man had spoken since they had met.

Hall said "All summer long, for two summers in a row." Between his freshman and sophomore years at the College of Charleston he cleaned hundreds of pounds of fish that the tourists caught on the charter boats. They often let him have some of the catch and he shared it with his friends at Fort Johnson.

The old man laughed and spat tobacco juice into the sink. When they had dressed all of the fish the old man looked out the window and spoke again.

"Dinner time's soon. We'd be blessed for you to join us," he said.

Hall declined the invitation, but didn't refuse a piece of pan-fried redfish stuffed inside a homemade biscuit. It was delicious and made him second guess his decision to leave.

On his way back out to the river, he relied on his instruments to help him navigate in the darkness and noticed a light in an old fishhouse that he had believed to be abandoned. A dump truck was pulling up to the dilapidated building and Hall wondered how soon the area would become the newest gated waterfront community. He ate the last bite of the biscuit and pointed his boat toward home, into the setting sun.

Chapter Fifteen

Gale used the bezel on her dive watch to mark the time when Arnold left. So far he had been gone for forty minutes. During that time she had explored her prison as much as her chain would allow. Before he left Arnold had closed the window by nailing a piece of plywood over the opening. It was dark inside the building, but her eyes had adjusted and there was enough light coming under the door and through the holes in the roof for her to see. The light was orange from the sunset, and she knew the weather was going to be good tomorrow.

Her restraint was simple, primitive, and escape proof. There was no way for her to free herself unless she amputated her foot. The heavy chain that was connected to the handcuffs was bolted to a steel girder that ran the length of the building. She considered trying to climb the chain to get to the bolts, but she could see that they were rusted in place and doubted that she could loosen them, even if she had the proper tools.

Arnold had been gone for two hours when she heard his small boat return. He burst through the door as if he expected her to be gone, breathing hard from his effort. She purposely sat facing away from the door and didn't turn toward him until she heard him approach.

"I got you some things," he said. He dropped two grocery bags on the floor in front of her and waited for her to look inside them. Gale made no effort to see what was in the bags. Arnold blinked first and went over to his lawn chair, opened a can of beer and turned on the small television set.

Gale opened the bags and found some clothing, a package of baby wipes, a towel, a stick of deodorant and a few other items. There were two warm up suits, sweatpants with matching tops. She must really smell bad for Arnold to have gotten her some clean clothing. She held the top against her body to see if it would fit.

"It'll fit." Arnold startled her when he spoke. He was close to her and she hadn't even heard him move across the room.

"You look like you're the same size as my sister and that's what I got her for Christmas last year."

What a lucky girl, Gale thought.

"Thanks, I appreciate it." She wanted to stay on his good side but didn't want to do anything he might misread.

"You can change clothes now," Arnold said.

He stepped toward her and she stiffened. The lid, her only weapon, was wrapped inside her blanket and every time he got close to her she realized how enormous he really was. He bent in front of her and took the handcuff off of her ankle and she saw that he put the key in the front pocket of his grimy blue jeans. He threw the empty beer can on the floor on his way out the door and closed it behind him.

Between the plywood covering and the window frame Gale could see his shadow. He was watching, waiting for her to take her clothes off. She felt the hot tears in the corner of her eyes and clenched her fists. No problem, asshole. She'd changed out of wet bathing suits on the beach so many times she had it down to a science. She draped the blanket over her shoulders and changed out of her shorts without taking her shoes off. The sweat pants were a little loose around her waist but she tied them with the drawstring. Then she pulled her shirt over her head without unbuttoning it, left her sports bra on and slipped on the sweatshirt. When she was finished changing she turned around and glanced at the window. He was still there. The door was several feet from the window. If she rushed toward the door she thought she could make it before he knew she was trying to escape. She could dive off the end of the dock and swim to shore or to the shallow marsh where he couldn't follow her in his boat. She took too long to decide.

Arnold burst through the door so quickly she screamed, and her scream scared him so badly that he screamed back at her. She screamed again when he grabbed her arm and pulled her toward a small closet. She hit him as hard as she could on the top of his head but he didn't even blink. After several blows her hand started to hurt, and she opened her hand to claw his face with her fingernails.

Every speaker she'd ever heard talk about personal security told women not to fight their attackers because a violent response usually meant the victim was hurt worse than they would have been if they were submissive. Separate your mind from your body and imagine anything to ignore what was really happening, she had always been told. But one speaker was different. She had been raped and told women to fight like hell. Scratch their eyes out. Bite their tongues off. She told them if they could tear twelve sheets of typing paper in half they were strong enough to rip an ear off of their attackers head.

She reached for his ear but he caught her by her wrist.

"He's here. Don't make any noise. He'll kill you this time," Arnold warned before he closed the closet door.

"Arnold!" Gale heard someone outside yell. She recognized the voice. It was the man she thought of as Blondie. The one with the knife. She held her breath.

"Since you're lying around on your ass I assume you fixed the boat," Blondie said when he walked into the building. He put a fresh six-pack in the cooler and took one back for himself.

"Yeah, sure," Arnold mumbled. "Have you got some money for me?" he asked Blondie.

"I told you you'd get paid when we finished. You nervous 'bout that bitch?"

Arnold nodded his head.

"Don't worry. They haven't found the body yet. The sharks and crabs she loved so much will take care of her. Back the truck up and dump the dirt into the barge. I want to drop another load and get back to town before it gets dark. That old truck doesn't have any taillights."

Arnold looked at the closet and hesitated.

"Go on. You know I can't back that thing," Blondie said.

Arnold shuffled out the door.

Gale was on her hands and knees watching through the space between the bottom of the door and the floor and lying as still as a stone with her cheek pushed against the dusty floor. She watched Blondie sit on the lounge chair and drink his beer, draining it in two gulps. He tossed the can on the floor and opened another one. While she watched he took a leather pouch out of his back pocket and set it beside him on the chair. There was a small glass pipe in the pouch, and he held a lighter to the end of it. He inhaled and held his breath until he started coughing and wheezing. Then he cursed and pounded on his chest with his fist.

She heard the truck start and then felt the vibrations as it backed down the wharf that was attached to the fish house. She relaxed a little when Blondie took another hit from the pipe and walked outside.

"All done. There's no more room in the boat," she heard Arnold say when they walked back inside. Arnold stared right at the closet.

"Yeah, let's go," Blondie said and stretched his arms above his head. Then he walked over and relieved himself through a hole in the floor. Both men walked back outside, and Arnold closed the door to the warehouse behind him.

Gale's heart was pounding when she heard the old marine diesel engine cough to life. Free from the chain she stood up and got ready to run, waiting to hear the old barge depart. She would go right through anyone who got in her way. Her hand was on the closet doorknob when she heard the warehouse door open, and Arnold came back inside. He opened the closet, and without saying anything he locked the handcuff around her ankle and went back outside.

Chapter Sixteen

Coming back from St. Helena Island, Hall slowed for the no wake zone in Skull Creek and looked over at the Lowcountry Seafood docks. He saw someone on one of the shrimp boats and decided to stop.

The fishing guide, the one who helped him free the dolphin and turned out to be Gale's brother, was working on one of the winches that hauled in the nets. His arms were greasy from his elbows to his fingers, and parts of the winch were strewn across the deck. He noticed Hall and gestured for him to come aboard.

"Did they have any luck today?" Hall asked.

"No," Silas answered. He didn't slow in his efforts, and Hall wondered if he had made a mistake by stopping to talk. While he worked in silence a great blue heron floated out of the night sky and landed on the gunwale of the boat, next to Silas. Its wingspan was as wide as Hall was tall. Silas picked up a small dead fish and threw it to the great bird, which caught the delicacy and gulped it into its long beak. Hall watched the bulge in the long, slender neck of the bird move downward until it disappeared into the bird's body.

"That's Gale's bird," Silas said. "She found him covered with oil one day out in the sound. He had lost so many feathers that he couldn't fly, so Gale nursed him back and fed him scraps when she helped me clean fish. Now I can't get rid of the damn thing. He flies in here all the time, expecting to get fed."

The large bird squawked loudly, almost as if it took issue with how he had been described. It made a few more noises and then lifted off the dock, flying low over the water toward Pinckney Island.

"I wonder if he knows she's gone," Hall said.

The two men watched Gale's bird until it disappeared into darkness. Hall broke the silence once again.

"Do you know where Gale was going yesterday?" he asked.

Silas shook his head.

"I know she planned to check on a waterfront development near Beaufort, but she mentioned she wanted to take you by there on the way to eat supper with Jimmy and Rebecca. Most likely she got a report from someone and went to check it out."

"Have you checked her office?" Hall asked.

"Yeah," Silas answered. He seemed embarrassed.

"Her journal was up to date, right up to the night before she disappeared."

Hall nodded his head and thought for a while. Then he had an idea.

"Did she have her own telephone line?" he asked.

"Yes," Silas said.

"Let's check something out," Hall said.

Silas unlocked the small office and Hall was saddened once again by the emptiness that existed where Gale should have been. He sat down at her desk and picked up the telephone receiver. He caught a whiff of her sweet scent when he put the phone to his ear.

"Do you know if anyone has used this since she disappeared?" Hall asked.

"I think I'm the only one who's been in here since she's been gone and I haven't used it," he answered.

Hall punched the star button and a two-digit code. He was connected to another line, and it began to ring. An older sounding woman answered the phone. After identifying himself, Hall asked the woman if she knew Gale Pickens.

"No, I don't believe I do," she answered.

Hall was about to hang up when she continued on with her previous sentence. Hall had mistaken her pause for an ending.

"The only Gale I know is that young lady who is working to keep our water free from pollution."

Biting his tongue to keep from interrupting the woman again, Hall learned she had called Gale the day before yesterday to report some dead fish floating in the water near her house. Hall began writing the directions down and realized she was describing the creek where he had collected the dead fish yesterday. Disheartened, he hung up the phone.

"She reported the fish kill I checked out yesterday," Hall said.

Silas nodded and looked out the window.

Hall continued to look over Gale's desk. He picked up a framed photograph and asked Silas who was standing next to Gale.

"That's Representative Horry. He helped pass new state-wide regulations about the use of fertilizers and pesticides on golf courses. The legislation passed, but he didn't get re-elected."

"Strong golf course lobby?" Hall asked.

"You could say that. The money in this county is on Hilton Head Island, the same place the high-dollar golf courses are. It's hard to keep the greens green in the middle of August without a little dye and other petro chemicals," Silas explained.

Hall considered the possibility. Could someone have gotten so upset over the new laws that they took revenge on Gale? Silas answered that question for him.

"The developers were smart enough to turn things around. The golf courses advertise that they are sixty per cent organic, the best percentage in the country. They forget to tell everyone it wasn't their idea."

"We're going to have a memorial service on Sunday at the old Sheldon Church," Silas continued. "She really liked you. I don't know if she ever told you that."

"I liked her a lot too," Hall said. He wished he'd told Gale.

They went back outside and Silas locked up the office. Persimmon clouds with cinnamon edges seemed reluctant to surrender to the twilight. The beauty of the sunset was too sensational to rush past, even as hungry and tired as he was. While Hall loitered on the dock he wondered if the display was a salute from God, a tribute to someone who cherished His creation and looked after it so well.

Chapter Seventeen

A t three a.m. the alarm clock blared for half a minute before Hall woke up. He stumbled to the dresser and turned it off, trying to remember why he had set it for such an inhuman hour. Then he noticed there was a dripping sound coming from the kitchen. That meant the roof was leaking again which meant it was raining. It took all of his discipline to keep from getting back underneath the warm, dry blankets.

A hot shower (inside) and two cups of coffee made him feel like a new man. He moved Belker's water bowl to catch the raindrops, and took his rain slicker off of the hook by the back door. During the spring and fall shrimping seasons he was expected to perform boardings and inspections of commercial fishing vessels. He needed to inspect a few more vessels by the end of the month. The state fishery agents also checked the commercial boats but had no authority to enforce federal regulations. The Georgia state line was less than ten miles away and a favorite tactic of captains wishing to avoid being stopped was to fish a zig-zag pattern back and forth between the two state boundaries. They were often surprised when a Fed stopped them. He knew his presence on the boats was tolerated only because the fishermen had no other choice. He understood their feelings. It was a little like driving around with a state trooper in your backseat.

The rain was steady and the sea rolling gently in the dark sound as he approached the Atlantic Ocean. He scanned the horizon with his binoculars, and saw the lights of a dozen shrimp boats. The coffee rumbled in his stomach and he wished that he would have eaten something before he left his house.

Miss Agnes was his first target. He pulled behind the boat when her nets were being brought in and hailed the captain on the radio. A line was thrown to him and he tied it to the bow cleat of his patrol boat. He timed his jump carefully, not wanting to go for a swim or get squashed between the two boats. He would check their harvest totals, Turtle Exclusion Devices, and federal and state fishing permits before he moved to another boat. If the boat seemed to be in poor condition he would check their safety equipment and report them to the Coast Guard if the boat didn't appear to be seaworthy. Once he was safely aboard the shrimp boat, the shrimpers would continue dragging their nets so the inspection would be as unobtrusive as possible.

The first stop was usually the most productive, because within minutes of boarding Miss Agnes every boat in the area would know that Hall was checking the shrimpers today. Jimmy once told him that he stayed in the cottage one rainy day and pretended to hail a shrimp boat on the marine radio. He knew anyone fishing illegally would high tail it out of the area and he didn't even have to leave his kitchen.

The deck crew of the Miss Agnes surprised him. Two of the four fishermen were women.

"Dis my wife, my dotter, and her husman," the old captain explained.

His daughter looked to be forty and his wife twenty years past that. Hall wondered how productive their day would be.

A novice waterman, Hall did not lie down and wake up with the weather. He saw only the rain and decided it was a rainy day. He failed to take into account the low pressure system that brought the rain also produced the accompanying wind and high seas. A few minutes on the internet checking the wave heights at a few of the offshore weather buoys before he left his house would have told him that it was a bit lumpy out on the open ocean today. Soon enough he would learn to live by the barometer as sailors before him had for centuries.

At twelve tons empty, the Miss Agnes went through the three foot high swells of Port Royal Sound with no rocking and very little spray coming over the bow. As soon as they cleared Joiner Bank and turned south they began to take the wind and waves on their port side however, and the old wooden ship began to creak and moan as she rolled back and forth. Hall struggled to keep his footing on the slippery deck as he walked from the pilothouse toward the stern of the boat. His shoes seemed unable to get any purchase on the wet deck.

"Keep your feet farther apart," the younger of the two women advised him when she walked past. He was amazed that she wasn't holding onto anything and was carrying a bundle of fishing net that was bigger than he was.

Even in calm seas the deck of a fishing boat is a dangerous place to be. Hall knew that and found a place to stay out of the way while the captain gathered his papers. The hold was empty, so there were no shrimp for him to estimate their catch. Gradually he acquiesced to the rhythm of the ocean and began to feel more comfortable. As the light began to build in the east he saw the hotels and condos on Hilton Head Island begin to emerge in the growing dawn.

Although the captain didn't touch the throttle, the old boat slowed to a crawl when the great nets were lowered into the ocean. Thick steel cables went from a large winch that was mounted amidships to two tall booms, one port and one starboard. Two large wooden "doors" were attached to the outer portion of each net and acted as planers, dragging the nets off of the deck and spreading them open in the water. The nets actually dragged the ocean floor which was only twenty-two feet below the surface this close to the shore. The location of every rocky outcropping or shipwreck in these waters was well known and avoided by the shrimpers, who dragged their nets with trepidation after a big storm moved a shipwreck or uncovered a stony projection.

The old diesel engine kept time with its steady beating. The waves breaking against the bow sounded like muted cymbals and the wind played the strings, singing and whistling through the rigging and lines. Hall thought it was mesmerizing.

After thirty minutes the powerful winches pulled in the nets, and the crew prepared to receive the bounty of the sea. Hall saw the captain shake his head and asked him what was wrong.

"Comin' up too fast," he answered.

Hall understood what he meant when he saw the mostly empty net. They harvested less than three bushels of shrimp and several dozen small fish. The small fish that fell from the net were crescent-shaped in death and missing their eyes. Hall recognized pinfish, juvenile snapper, and many mullet. He walked over and picked one up.

"Why didn't the crabs eat these fish?" Hall asked out loud.

"Dunno, Bossman," the son in law of the captain said. "Mebbe dey don taste no good."

He didn't have any evidence bags with him so he collected two fish from each species and put three in one of the pockets of his rain coat and three in the other pocket. He took a notepad made of waterproof paper out of his shirt pocket and scribbled down two pages of notes. With the boat now pitching and rolling he thought anyone reading them would have thought he was drunk when he was writing. He glanced inside the wheelhouse, but didn't see a GPS display or a depth finder. The only electronics were an ancient marine radio and a brand new color television that was tuned to the local morning newscast. He looked at the shoreline and did his best to estimate where he was.

When he was finished taking notes Hall watched the male crewmen use an aluminum grain shovel to scoop up the fish and throw them overboard. A single common tern among a screech of laughing gulls dove and tried to pluck one of the dead mullet out of the water. The fish was too heavy for the small bird so he dropped it and chased one of the seagulls, trying to snatch a piece of its meal from its beak. Hall checked on his boat as it bobbed up and down behind them, close enough to the stern of the shrimp boat to stay clear of the nets.

While the nets were in the water they steadied the boat by softening the rolling from side to side, and all Hall had to contend with was the up and down movement as the trawler crested and broke through the oncoming waves. Now, with the nets out of the water, the boat pitched sharply from side to side in addition to the up and down movement. He knew that the stern of the boat moved the least, and he moved to the back of the boat and tried to focus on the horizon. His mouth was dry and tasted like stale coffee, and the tiny buildings on shore went up and down, up and down. This was a lot different than being in the protected inshore waters in his small boat.

The nausea wasn't overwhelming until they changed course and ran with the wind. The exhaust fumes hung in the air and traveled with the boat. Hall struggled for a breath of fresh air, but the combined effect of movement and diesel fumes put him over the edge. He barely made it to the back railing of the shrimp boat before he spewed.

Mercifully, the crew ignored him until he was done throwing up. Hall wiped his mouth on the wet sleeve of his rain slicker and wished he was back on solid ground. Like anyone else who had ever been seasick, he just wanted everything to quit moving. Too embarrassed to go back into the cabin, he stayed out on deck and tried to keep his face in the wind, which seemed to help a little. The captain's wife came outside and gave him a jelly jar full of ice water and a sympathetic smile.

"You ain't the first to get sick on dis old boat," she said.

Hall thanked her and looked behind the shrimp boat at the dark wake that trailed behind them. Then he noticed that he had puked all over the front of his patrol boat.

Hall overheard the captain talking with another shrimper on the marine radio and soon they drew near several other shrimp boats. To his great relief, the boat steadied when the nets were let back down. Everyone on board saw the good catches of the neighboring boats and was anxious to check their nets. After what seemed like an eternity, the nets were hauled back in.

Even Hall could tell the nets were recovered much slower than before. The rigging groaned under the stress of a good catch, and soon over a ton of shrimp was wriggling and sliding across the slippery deck. Hall struggled to write down some notes while the ship pitched and heaved. The crew was all business, shoveling the valuable cargo into the belly of the ship.

Three more times Hall got sick over the side of the boat. The last time it was only dry heaves and if he remembered correctly from his early college days, his gut would be sore tomorrow. The other casualty of the day was his shoes. Looking at his ruined leather docksiders, covered with shrimp parts, fish blood, and vomit he understood why the fishermen all wore white rubber boots.

It stopped raining before he got home, and everything that was plastered to the front deck and windshield of his patrol boat was dry and stuck on like glue. A dolphin surfaced in the channel near his dock and chirped at him. This time he was certain it was the same one because it had the scar on its back near its dorsal fin. He could understand why people found it hard to resist the urge to feed the friendly creatures.

It took him an hour and a half to remove everything that had once been in his stomach from his boat. After putting his ruined shoes in a trash can he walked barefoot to his cottage and picked up three sand burrs for his trouble, one of them lodging in the fresh cut in his instep.

He showered outside in his clothes again then remembered he didn't have any more fresh uniforms to change into. When he took off his wet pants his cell phone fell out of the pocket and clattered on the concrete and oyster shell floor of the shower. He flipped it open and the screen was blank with no signs of life. He doubted if a biologist ever had a morning like this.

The phone in the cottage still worked, and after answering its ring he drove his patrol truck to the visitors' parking lot to meet a lady whose station wagon had been broken into. He was wearing a pair of gym shorts and a US Fish and Wildlife Service sweatshirt since he didn't have any clean uniforms, and she made him show her his identification before she would believe he was an officer. Someone had smashed a window in her car and took a GPS unit that had been attached to the windshield with a suction cup. He took all of the information from her that he needed for his report and gave her the case number for her insurance company.

She said "You people should let everyone know it's not safe to leave things in your car here." It was clear to Hall that she believed her loss to be his fault. He pointed to a sign posted in front of her car with that exact warning.

"You should make the sign bigger," she said as she drove away.

Chapter Eighteen

All morning long the rain had beaten down on the tin roof of the old fish house. Puddles on the floor that corresponded with the holes in the roof, and Gale had to move her bedroll three times to keep it dry. After Arnold and Blondie left yesterday, and she was certain that the old barge was far enough away, she called for help. After her voice gave out she beat on the floor with a piece of wood until her hands were tired and swollen. No one heard her. It was hot now in the old building since the clouds lifted and the sun filled the air with humidity.

No matter how hard she tried she could not reach the window or the door. The chain allowed her a circle of movement that kept her several feet from all of the walls. More than once she saw rats scatter around the room or run across one of the rafters, but it wasn't the four legged vermin that concerned her. She looked everywhere but couldn't find anything small enough to try to pick the handcuff lock with. There was a pile of electrical wiring next to the television that looked promising, but it might as well have been the key itself. It was too far away. She would have to wait until she was free from the chain to make her escape.

Arnold had checked on her twice this morning. He was working on the barge again, and if she understood the shouts and threats correctly, the doors on the bottom of the barge would not completely close after they dumped the load of contaminated soil yesterday. She heard Blondie leave in the truck late last night and hoped he wouldn't come back, but knew that he probably would.

Something moved in the corner of the room, and she turned her head to see what it was. She thought it was another rat but soon realized it was a small, skinny kitten. She opened a can of Vienna sausages Arnold gave her and eased toward the skittish cat. Gale put the can on the floor, sat next to it and hummed quietly, waiting to see if he would come closer.

Within a few minutes the kitten was eating out of the can, and a few minutes after that he was purring in Gale's arms. She couldn't believe how much better she felt now that she had a friend. She wished she could train it to be an attack cat.

Suddenly Arnold burst through the door and the kitten shot out of her arms.

"He's back!" he said.

Just like he had before, Arnold unlocked the handcuff and led her to the closet.

"Just remember, he'll kill us both if he finds you," he warned.

Gale took up her position on the dirty floor, staring under the door. She saw Blondie come inside the fish house, and heard him curse Arnold when he found out the barge wasn't fixed yet.

"Then drive your ass to Beaufort and get the part you need!" Blondie thundered when Arnold tried to explain.

Gale saw Arnold leave the building and Blondie go back outside, then she heard a car start.

"Get me something to eat," Blondie yelled, and Gale knew she was not being left alone.

After hearing and seeing nothing for a few minutes Gale couldn't stand it any longer. She eased open the closet door and quietly walked over to the window. Blondie was lying on his back on the dock with his ball cap pulled down over his eyes. His chest rose and fell in a regular rhythm.

The first thing Gale did was examine the pile of wires and junk on the floor. She found a few pieces that looked promising and put them in her pocket. Before she could do anything else she felt someone walking across the wooden planks and hurried back to the closet.

Gale didn't get the door to the closet closed fast enough, but apparently Blondie was blinded by walking from the bright sunshine into the dark building and didn't see her close the door. Once again she resumed her posture of lying on the floor and watching underneath the door. She took the sharp metal lid out of her pocket and clenched it in her hand.

Blondie scratched himself, burped, and slumped in the reclining lawn chair, the only piece of furniture in the building. He looked far less imposing than she remembered him being. Even though her jaw still ached whenever she moved her mouth she began to think about attacking him.

Gale could count the days of her life that she had been sick on one hand. She never slept more than six hours a night and always had too many projects going at one time. Ever since she had been a child she knew that life was what she made of it, and she had decided to make the most out of it. She had fought against people who wanted to hurt the land and water for their own profit. She was ready to fight now. As a teenager just out of high school she set sail on a mercy ship for a voyage around the world. By the time most of her friends were starting their sophomore year of college she had delivered babies and held the hands of the dying.

And now her life was threatened. Gale believed she would rather die trying to escape than suffer abuse at their hands. It had to be now. She couldn't do anything when she was shackled to the chain. Blondie looked like he was dozing. She might get lucky and make it past him before he realized what was happening. If she could just make it outside, she knew he'd never catch her. She quietly stood and stretched her leg muscles. A muscle cramp now would be fatal.

While she stretched her quads and calf muscles she remembered the handcuff that was dangling from her left ankle. It would be noisy, banging along the ground as she ran, but she didn't think that it would make her fall. She was ready.

On her hands and knees she peeked out under the door once again. Blondie was still in the lawn chair. One arm was hanging limply beside him and his mouth was wide open. She stood and began to open the closet door as quietly as she could. Just when the door was opened wide enough for her to see out of, it creaked loudly on its hinges. Blondie stirred from his sleep and Gale froze in place.

After minutes that seemed like hours, and aged her in years, Blondie appeared to drift back to sleep. Just when she was ready to try to open the door a little wider the door squeaked again. Blondie heard it too. She watched him rub his unshaven face and look around, trying to find the source of the noise.

Gale gripped her feeble weapon tightly in her fingers and stepped back against the wall of the closet. As soon as his hand touched the door handle she would explode against the door and knock him to the floor. She would be two hundred yards away before he got back to his feet. When she gritted her teeth a painful reminder of this man's brutality shot through her jaw.

"Where did you come from?" Blondie asked.

With that simple question Gale felt the strength begin to sag from her coiled legs and arms. How had he seen her? She didn't care anymore. She would fight until it was over. As she steeled herself against the opening of the door she heard another sound that brought terror to her heart.

The sick, mechanical sound of a switchblade opening was etched forever in her memory. She knew the man standing on the other side of the door had his knife in his hand again, and was ready to use it. She watched his shadow spill between the door and the doorframe and held her breath.

"Maybe if you'd eat some of the damn mice around here you wouldn't be so skinny."

Gale had to concentrate to keep from hyperventilating. The man who thought he had already killed her was standing less than two feet away, talking to the stray kitten.

"C'mere, cat. I won't hurt ya."

When the shadow moved away from the door Gale sank to her knees and peeked around the door frame. Blondie was near the middle of the building, trying to coax the kitten to come close to him. Much to her surprise, it went to the killer.

With much curiosity Gale watched the violent man stroke the small animal with tenderness and rub its head between his ears. He carried it back to his chair, and held him in his lap. They sat there together until Blondie tried to light a cigarette. Blondie shrieked when the frightened kitten sank his claws into his groin. He danced around the room with the now terrified kitten clinging to his crotch. The sharp claws had easily gone through his khaki pants and were drawing blood. The switchblade flashed in his hand once again, and he swung it at the defenseless kitten.

He misjudged the scrambling creature and Gale saw a seam of crimson flow from the tip of the knife across his leg. He finally managed to backhand the kitten off of him and it landed next to his lounge chair with a muffled thud, sounding like a shoe dropped on the floor. The kitten tried to stand and walk but he was woozy from spinning round and round with Blondie and teetered on unstable legs. Blondie picked up the kitten and stroked him a few times. Then he severed its head with his switchblade and squeezed it, watching the blood spurt from its neck and flow down over his hand.

Gale sobbed and bit her hand to keep from being heard. She slumped to the floor and pulled the closet door shut when Blondie walked out of the building.

Chapter Nineteen

His "formal" uniform, long-sleeved polyester shirt, clip-on tie and pat-
ent leather shoes, was much more uncomfortable than his everyday
work uniform. Fortunately the courtroom was well air-conditioned and cool to the
point of making his sweat-dampened shirt feel chilly. Hall had been here only once
before, accompanying Jimmy when he met with the county solicitor to discuss a
proposed plea bargain in an upcoming trial.

He saw the deputy that had taken his prisoner to jail a few days ago and sat down
next to him. Hall relaxed a little when the deputy told him nothing was likely to
happen since this was the defendant's first appearance.

"I'm sure his attorney will continue the case a few times, waiting for the time
when you or the victim doesn't show up. Then he'll tell the judge that he's ready to
try the case, and the solicitor will have to dismiss, since there's no witnesses present," the deputy said.

Hall looked around and saw the girl who had been assaulted. She was sitting
with an older couple he supposed to be her parents. The suspect sat on the other
side of the courtroom, next to two men, one of whom had a briefcase on his lap. His
attorney, Hall guessed. He made a mental note never to miss court.

The docket full of domestic assaults, traffic charges, and other misdemeanor
crimes bored the other law enforcement officer to tears, but Hall was fascinated.
He had never been in a court session before and was amazed and confused at how
things were done. While the solicitor called one case and read the formal charges,
her two assistants whispered with defense attorneys, working out last minutes deals
and pleas. The judge was often engaged in different conversations with a defense

attorney, the solicitor, and his clerk. Police officers, deputy sheriffs, and highway patrolmen testified about the grimy details of their cases: how many stitches the assault victim received, what the blood-alcohol level of the drunk driver was, and what verbal or physical abuse the defendant had given them. Their testimony was short and to the point.

Hall tried to rehearse in his mind what he would say when the judge asked him what happened. He made a few scribbles in his notebook, phrases and terms he heard the other cops use. The mock court he had participated in during his training had not prepared him for this.

During a recess one of the assistant solicitors approached him.

"Did you bring a copy of the statute with you?' he asked.

"Excuse me?" Hall was confused.

"We· don't deal much with the game and fish laws, so Jimmy always brought a copy of the statutes with him," the attorney for the state said.

Before Hall could speak the deputy next to him answered.

"He's with me. CCW and underage possession of alcohol. No fish and game stuff today"

The solicitor looked at his notes.

"Hazelton is representing him. I'm sure he'll ask for a continuance."

At about the time Hal assumed court would be adjourned for lunch, the attorney who represented his defendant stood and asked the judge for permission to speak.

"Your Honor, I am scheduled to appear before the legislature this afternoon and I was hoping to take care of this matter before I return to the capitol."

The deputy next to Hall whispered in his ear and told him who Ambrose Hazelton was, the former law partner of Hewlitt Sands. Hall recognized Sands as the top prosecutor in the county. The judge instructed the solicitor to call the case.

Hall didn't realize what was happening until the deputy got up and sat down at the prosecutor's table and motioned for him to sit beside him. The solicitor read the charges against the defendant.

"Carrying a concealed weapon and possession of alcohol by a person less than twenty-one years of age. How does the defendant plead?"

"Brandon Rodgers pleads not guilty, your Honor," Mr. Hazelton answered.

Hall McCormick and the deputy rose from their seats and placed their left hands on the Bible and raised their right hands. The clerk of court swore them in and Hall took the stand.

In district, or misdemeanor court, Hall knew there was no jury. The judge listened to the evidence and made a decision. Any appeals were remanded to superior court for a jury trial. Hall looked at the judge and began to testify.

He related the facts of the case in the briefest way possible, just as he had seen the other officers do all morning. When he was finished, the deputy briefly spoke and the prosecution rested.

"The defense calls Katrina Wellsley," Ambrose Hazelton said.

The teenaged girl Hall had seen the defendant pawing at walked down the aisle in the middle of the courtroom with her head hanging low. Hall looked at her, but she never looked up. She was sworn in by the clerk and took her seat in the witness stand.

"Miss Wellsley, do you remember coming to my office and giving me a sworn statement?" Hazleton asked.

She nodded her head, and the judge told her she had to give a verbal answer.

"Yes sir," she said. Hall could barely hear her answer.

"Do you remember telling me you got the bottle of liquor from the restaurant where you worked?"

"Yes, sir."

"And do you remember telling me it was your idea for my client to give you a ride home that night?"

"Yes, sir."

"No more questions, your Honor."

The solicitor shook her head when the judge asked her if she wanted to question the witness.

"You may step down, Miss Wellsley."

The defense called the defendant's father who testified that his son was driving his car, and that it was the father's pistol that was under the seat.

"Brandon had no idea the gun was there, your Honor. It was my mistake, not his," he concluded.

"Counselor, unless you have any other evidence to present, I'm inclined to dismiss the charges," the judge said to the solicitor.

"I have no other evidence to present."

"Case dismissed," the judge said.

"That's it?" Hall asked the deputy sitting next to him. He just shrugged his shoulders. Hall left the courtroom and tried to find the girl. He knew she had lied. He caught up to her and her parents in the parking lot.

"Miss Wellesley, can I talk to you?" Hall asked.

Her father stopped and turned around, while the girl and her mother kept walking.

"Officer, I heard you're new around here. My daughter shouldn't have put herself in that situation. Brandon would have never done the things you said that he did. His father is an important person around here, someone that matters. I don't want you to talk to my daughter. If you try, I'll report you to your supervisor," he said.

The girl lied. Her parents knew it, probably told her to do it. Hire a high-powered attorney, and buy a quick dismissal. He wondered what was at stake.

While he watched them drive away, a sports car pulled up behind him and beeped its horn. The driver, who had just been exonerated of all charges against him, rolled down his window and gave Hall a one-fingered salute.

Hall took off his tie and rolled up his sleeves. When he got to his truck he had to open both doors to let the heat escape before he got behind the wheel. The bad taste in his mouth contrasted sharply with the sweet smell of jasmine from the vines that ringed the municipal parking lot. He was pissed off and disappointed but believed no matter what just happened he had been in the right place at the right time and had done the right thing. He had been alive long enough to realize that money and status seldom protected someone forever.

After the cab of the truck cooled down a little he climbed in and slammed the door. When he reached down to buckle his seat belt he heard a hiss like a snake and his face felt like it was on fire! As he jumped out of the cab of his truck, the seatbelt tangled around one of his arms and in his blindness he fell to his knees, sneezing and coughing at the same time. He felt the snot and mucous pour out of his nose and slide down onto his lips and chin. A strong hand clamped onto his arm and pulled him to his feet.

"Hold on a second, I've got some water."

Hall felt the cool, soothing water splash onto his face and in a few seconds he could make out his rescuer through teary eyes. The tall, black man in a gray uniform told Hall the same thing he'd been told in training.

"Don't rub your eyes, you'll make it worse."

Hall nodded his understanding because he couldn't yet speak. He turned his face into the feeble breeze, and it seemed to help.

"Thanks," Hall wheezed when he was able to.

The man he thanked was a full foot taller than Hall was and his shoulders were so wide it looked like he was wearing a lineman's shoulder pads under his highway patrol uniform.

"Are you gonna be OK?" the trooper asked.

Hall said. "I think so. That was pretty stupid of me."

The trooper walked away smiling, and Hall looked at the can of oleoresm capsi-cum on his pistol belt. He must have snagged the seatbelt buckle on the lip of the canister when he tried to buckle it, and sent a burst of the powerful pepper spray straight into his face. The first person he'd ever used force against was himself.

Chapter Twenty

As much as Varnum disliked wearing a coat and tie to work everyday he hated wearing his uniform even more. He had been a detective for twelve years, and it seemed like every time he put on his uniform it fit a little tighter around his waist, and the Kevlar vest was a little smaller. Today was his day off and he was moonlighting, directing traffic at a construction site. The dust from earthmoving equipment stuck to his sweaty face, and there were damp crescents of sweat under his armpits. Next semester's tuition was due next week, and unless he wanted a very disappointed daughter on his conscience he needed to earn a few extra dollars. After eight hours in the sun he was finished and pulled into the nearest stop-and-rob for a cold drink.

He went into the store, nodded to the clerk and walked past a sign that said "employees only". After he used the bathroom he opened the door to the cooler and stepped inside. He learned this trick when he was a road deputy, working long hours in the Carolina heat and humidity. From inside the cooler he could look out over the bottles of soda and beer and see who came and went while his core temperature returned to normal. He unbuttoned his shirt, hooked a finger behind the vest at the top of his sternum and pulled it away from his sweaty t-shirt, letting the cold air cool him down. He was getting ready to leave the cooler and buy a bottle of water when he saw someone he recognized walk into the store.

Calvin Jackson Jr. was the first second-generation criminal Varnum had ever arrested. Less than one month out of the academy Varnum was riding with his training officer when they responded to a report of domestic violence. The address was a regular call for service, his trainer had told him, and the Jackson family was good for at least one knock-down-drag-out family fight every month. Varnum worked his first homicide that night and never forgot the sight of a two year old boy in a high chair with his daddy sitting beside him at the kitchen table eating supper when they walked into the small house. Mrs. Jackson was lying on the kitchen floor with a steak knife buried in her chest. "DRT" his training officer said later, "Dead Right There".

Fourteen years later Varnum worked his first case as a detective, a sixteen-year-old kid that had been caught driving a stolen car. He went into the interview room and couldn't get the suspect to admit to anything. When he read the name on the arrest sheet he remembered. The only thing that surprised him more was when the boy's father came to pick him up at the station. Dad had served ten years of a twenty-year sentence for second degree murder and was living with his son in the same house where he'd killed his wife.

Calvin Jackson Jr. was stoned out of his mind. He walked like he had a spring in his left Air Jordan and a five pound weight in his right one. Varnum watched as his eyes swept the store lingering at each surveillance camera, judging their coverage areas. He opened the cooler door in front of Varnum, grabbed a thirty-two ounce bottle of malt liquor and shoved it down the front of his baggy shorts. Then he went to the register, bought a single cigar, and walked outside. He was pulling all of the tobacco out of the cigar when Varnum walked up to him.

"Are you so stoned that you didn't see my car, Mr. Jackson?"

Calvin didn't recognize the detective and didn't like the fact that this cop knew his name. He started to walk away.

"You're under arrest," Varnum said and grabbed his arm. Calvin Jackson pulled away from him which Varnum had anticipated. Using his momentum against him Varnum shoved him and kicked his legs out from underneath him at the same time. He landed on top of his arrestee and was putting the handcuffs on him when Calvin started screaming.

"Calm down, nobody's going to hurt you." But the young man kept screaming and was trying to buck Varnum off of him.

Varnum rolled him on his side and started searching him. In one of his pants pocket was a small bag of weed. Varnum tossed it onto the hood of his car and rolled him onto his other side. He found a lighter and some change in his other pocket and pulled everything out. There was blood on his hand when he pulled it out of the pocket.

"Shit."

He left his prisoner screaming on the hot asphalt and unlocked his unmarked police car. There was a bottle of hand sanitizer in his glove box and he used half of it to clean his hands. Then he called for an ambulance and a marked patrol car to transport his arrestee to the jail.

Calvin had rolled over and was sitting up. Varnum grabbed his shoulder and told him to stand up.

"What the hell is wrong with you?" Varnum asked.

"I'm hurt man, down there." There were tears in his eyes when he spoke.

Varnum saw the dark stain at his crotch and remembered the bottle of beer. He pulled on the waistband of the shorts and looked down. Calvin's boxer shorts were a mixture of broken glass, beer and blood.

"I think you cut your dick off," Varnum said.

Calvin's legs gave out on him and he fell back down on the ground.

When two other deputies and the paramedics arrived they took the handcuffs off of Calvin and used two pair of heavy-duty nylon straps to secure him to the gurney. Then the medics cut off his shorts.

Three cops, the convenience store clerk and two paramedics all said "ooooohhhh" at the same time and turned away from the spectacle. Calvin's manhood was attached to the rest of his body by the smallest thread of flesh. He stopped screaming when he saw everyone's reaction.

"What? What's wrong?" he asked.

"Nothing at all," one of the medics said. "You're gonna be fine. If you got any condoms stashed away you can give them to your friends. You ain't gonna need them anymore."

Calvin was still screaming when they loaded him in the back of the ambulance.

Varnum was just thinking that there might not be a Calvin Jackson III when he saw a black Trans Am cruise by. A white guy with blonde, almost white hair was driving it. He told one of the deputies that he needed to find out who was driving that car, and the two marked cars pulled the Trans Am over a few blocks away. They checked the driver's license and insurance and confirmed that the tag belonged on the car and then turned the driver loose. They came back to the convenience store and gave the information to Varnum.

"He's headed to the emergency room. Got a nasty looking cut on his leg. He said his knife slipped when he was cleaning some fish but it sure looked like somebody sliced him," the deputy said.

The name of the driver of the Trans Am was the same guy he had started a file on the day before, the parolee. Varnum thanked the deputies for their help and drove to his office instead of going home. It wasn't like anyone was waiting for him to come home anyway. When an arrestee was hospitalized there was a lot of paperwork to complete. Varnum took off his uniform shirt and bullet proof vest and hung them over the back of his chair. Before he started his report, he logged on the computer and checked his account and saw that he had three more views but no private messages. Maybe he needed to put a different picture on his profile. He decided that was too much trouble and got back to work.

Chapter Twenty One

The blow stung, and the sound of it rang through the fishouse. Blood dribbled onto the dirty wooden floor, but the victim offered no defense.

"You can go just as easy as that bitch did, Arnold," Blondie threatened. "All I have to do is toss you over and watch you sink like a rock."

Arnold did not know how to swim and it was his misfortune that Blondie knew that. The simple act of pretending to push him over the side brought the man to his knees. Although physically smaller and weaker than Arnold, Blondie intimidated his partner with ease, just like how he kept milking Mark Lancaster for more and more money.

All Arnold had done to cause the assault and death threat was report that the part needed to fix the stubborn hydraulic system was unavailable until the following day. It wasn't his fault, but Blondie didn't care. Blondie didn't really care that the boat couldn't be fixed for another day. He was just an asshole who liked to hurt people.

Ever since they had met in prison Blondie had been the boss, and Arnold preferred it that way. Someone to line up the jobs, someone to collect the money, someone to turn in if he got caught. Blondie needed Arnold to fix the boat and drive it, and Arnold needed the money. Blondie planned to dump his partner, literally, as soon as his usefulness expired.

Risking a glance at the closet, Arnold hoped Blondie wasn't going to stay overnight. Suddenly the blood was pounding in his ears. Blondie had been asleep when he got back from Beaufort. What if the girl had escaped while he was gone? The police would be here very soon if that had happened, he knew. If she escaped he hoped that Blondie did stay. Otherwise, he would take the rap for kidnapping and attempted murder all alone.

The tension built for thirty minutes. It climaxed when Arnold heard the sound of a boat motor. Risking a look out of the window, he saw two men in a camouflaged jon boat spreading a net across the creek. He and Blondie went outside and watched the men work until the mosquitoes drove them back into the fishhouse.

"I'm getting the hell out of here. I'll pick up the hose in the morning on my way out here." Blondie left in his Trans Am.

As soon as the car was out of sight Arnold rushed to the closet. Gale shielded her eyes from the flashlight, and Arnold let out a great sigh of relief.

"I thought you'd gotten away," he said.

Gale didn't respond. When her eyes adjusted she noticed the way that the filthy man was looking at her.

"You'll have to kill me first," Gale croaked. Her throat was dry, and her voice was convincing.

Arnold remembered the men with the fishing nets were close enough to hear a woman scream.

"I'm not going to do anything to you," he said.

"Why don't you let me go?"

"I can't. Not until we're finished. Then I'll leave and call the police and tell them where to find you," Arnold said.

Arnold backed away from the door to emphasize his good intentions. Gale wiped her eyes on her shirtsleeve and stood up, being careful not to let her guard down. Arnold hoped when he left she'd want to go with him but he knew it wasn't the right time to ask. He needed to lay more groundwork.

"I brought back some more things for you," Arnold said.

He gave her a jacket and another blanket he had bought for her in Beaufort.

"I thought you got cold the other night," Arnold said.

"Thanks," Gale whispered.

Arnold hoped her gratitude was just the beginning.

"Why are you guys dumping all that crap in the water? You know you're killing all the fish and crabs and everything else it touches."

Arnold's response was exactly what Gale expected, the same thing people told her when she yelled at them at a stoplight for throwing their cigarette butt on the ground or a developer when she complained about the muddy runoff from their construction sites.

"The little bit of stuff that we're doing doesn't make that big a difference."

"Everybody makes a difference, Arnold, either for good or for bad. Do you really want to leave this earth in worse shape than it was when you got here?"

Arnold just shrugged his shoulders. He walked over to the television and turned it on.

"Your friend killed my cat," she said. Arnold did not seem surprised.

"He's not my friend. We just do some things together. As soon as we're done with this stuff I'm outta here. I'd leave now, but he won't give me any of the money he owes me."

Arnold came back to her and apologized when he put the handcuff back on her ankle.

"Do you really think he's going to pay you later? What's going to stop him from leaving with the money and telling the cops where to find you?"

Chapter Twenty-Two

H all drove his work truck to the funeral service but wore civilian clothes, a pair of khaki pants and a shirt Gale had said she liked when they went out to dinner just two weeks ago. She had worn a blue tank top and her hair smelled like jasmine, he remembered. Hall had to park quite a way from the church because of all the other cars, and the service had already started when he arrived. When he walked through the old wrought iron gate a young woman handed him a memorial folder that had Gale's picture on the front of it, and she was as pretty as the picture in his mind. On the back of the folder was a quote from Rachel Carson.

"For all at last returns to the sea -- to Oceanus, the ocean river, like the everflowing stream of time, the beginning and the end."

Below the quote was information on how to make a donation to the Soundkeeper Project in memoriam, and a note indicating the paper was recycled. Hall thought Gale would have liked that very much.

Sheldon Church was not quite what Hall had expected. Round columns made from tabby bricks rose twenty feet into the air, and live oak trees adorned with Spanish moss towered three times higher. The huge windows of the church had rounded tops of the Greek revival style that would have reached to the roof if there had been a roof on the church. Hall didn't know that a local Tory burned the church in 1779, and after it was rebuilt in 1826 it lasted a scant thirty-nine years before Sherman burned it on his infamous march to the sea. Graves were scattered here and there which added to the solemn feeling in the air.

There looked to be two-hundred mourners gathered on the church grounds. A small podium had been erected underneath one of the spreading oaks, and a man

Hall didn't recognize was talking about Gale's love of the sea, her love of life. In a nice way he boasted about hiring her to be the first Port Royal Soundkeeper, knowing she was born to the job. Hall realized that he had been more than Gale's employer, he had been her friend.

Several others spoke, and Hall saw Silas sitting with Gale's father and a woman he assumed was Gale's mother. The older couple held each others' hands and nodded while Gale was remembered. Among the mourners Hall thought that he recognized a state senator and an anchorwoman from the local news. He knew that he was lucky to have known her, even for such a short time, and he couldn't help but wonder what might have been.

A choir comprised of schoolchildren sang a hymn at the end of the service, and Hall drifted over to the ruins of the church to get a better look and because he wasn't ready to leave. Even though he had seen only one person he knew, he felt that he was surrounded by friends. Someone touched him on his shoulder and he turned and saw Jimmy Barnwell and his wife. Hall bent down and gave Rebecca a hug.

"I always thought you two might hit it off," she said. Hall only smiled and nodded.

"Are you two ready to set sail?" Hall asked.

"We are," Jimmy replied. "The radar is fixed and tomorrow we'll finish our provisioning. We should be on Chesapeake Bay by the end of the month."

Jimmy took Hall by the elbow and led him a few steps away from his wife.

"If they find.....anything, please let me know. Gale was so careful on the water. I just don't understand how this happened." Jimmy said.

Hall promised to stay in touch and then made his way over to Gale's family. Silas shook his hand and introduced Hall to his mother. He told her how sorry he was for her loss and wished that he had something more to say. He'd only been to one or two funerals in his life and didn't have much experience in situations like this. Gale's father said that he didn't recognize Hall without his uniform on, which Hall was glad to hear but didn't understand.

On the way home from the memorial service Hall stopped by the cell phone store and bought a new phone. Even though he had to dip into his savings account to pay for it he was too embarrassed to submit a request for reimbursement to his supervisor. He didn't want to tell her that he had dropped it while he was in the shower and he didn't want to lie to her. He also went to the hardware store and bought a pair of white rubber boots like the shrimpers wore, planning ahead for the next time he hitchhiked on a shrimp boat.

Before he went home he drove down a familiar road he had not driven in more than a year. He parked his truck and took a small cooler inside of the laboratory building of the Waddell Mariculture Center. The familiar smells of chemicals, salt water, and fish greeted him when he walked past the reception area and into the hallway that led to where the different labs were located. Once upon a time he had worked here in this building and lived nearby in an old plantation house on Victoria Bluff overlooking the Colleton River that had been converted to student housing. All of the lab work for his thesis had been completed here, but even though his studies were specific to the reproductive cycle of the spottail bass, he had helped other students and researchers with their projects which ranged from artificially seeding oyster beds to studies on the endangered Atlantic sturgeon.

The Waddell Mariculture Center was one of the preeminent marine aquaculture centers in the world. In addition to the laboratory building, there were dozens of saltwater ponds and tanks that ranged from fifty gallons to over an acre in size. Experiments were conducted to determine if artificial light could be used to induce sexual maturity in shrimp at an earlier life stage and thereby increase their commercial feasibility. Cobia were raised in large tanks to be released into the wild to augment natural stocks. One pond was set aside to study the sexual maturity rate in pacific white shrimp. These surroundings were so much more familiar to him than a courtroom, and he enjoyed recording research data a whole lot more than writing citations.

Cliff Anderson was in a small room that was crammed with specimen bottles, test tubes, and microscopes. He was speaking with another biologist, and Hall waited until his friend noticed him.

"Look what the cat dragged in." Cliff took one of his latex gloves off and shook Hall's hand.

"It's good to see you too," Hall said.

Cliff had been awarded his masters degree a semester before Hall and was the last staff biologist hired before personnel restrictions were implemented. Under his lab apron he was wearing a pair of khaki shorts and Birkenstock sandals. Hall thought he looked a lot more comfortable in his work attire than Hall felt in his uniform.

"Did you bring me a few cold ones?" he asked Hall when he noticed the cooler.

"No, but that would have been a good idea. I need some help, if you've got the time."

Hall showed his friend the specimens he had collected when he was on the Miss Agnes.

"I'd like to see what toxins are present. We've had a few small fish kills recently, and if I can isolate the specific chemicals present I might be able to figure out who or what is poisoning them."

"You guys don't have your own lab?" Cliff asked.

"We do, but it's in Oregon and it might take more than a month to get the results back to me. I'm going to send some of the specimens to them so I can have a certified analysis that can be entered into court. I just want to know where to start looking."

"Do you want to do it? I have some undergrad students here that can take care of it, but if you want to do it yourself, make yourself at home."

The temptation was strong, but it would have been like going out on a date with someone who told you a month ago they just wanted to be friends.

"Can I take a rain check on that?" Hall asked.

"Of course."

Hall handed the frozen fish to his friend but kept one of the mullet in his cooler.

The two friends caught up with each other for a while and gossiped about mutual friends and where everyone went after grad school. It seemed like everyone landed a job as a biologist except for him.

"Nelson sold out," Cliff told him. "He tried to get a job back in Mississippi but the state wasn't hiring. He got a job with National Paper in Georgia, conducting water quality surveys and supervising their wetland remediation projects in the southeast. He told me he'd already paid off his student loans and bought a condo on a golf course."

Nelson. The one that dressed like a model from GQ and surprised everyone when he received his degree. Gainfully employed as a biologist.

Cliff told him he'd send him the test results as soon as he could and walked Hall out to his truck.

"There's a chance we might be able to fill some of our vacancies in the new fiscal year," Cliff said. Hall asked his friend to keep him informed and left the campus.

When he got home he took off his court uniform and changed into his brown uniform pants and a short sleeved polo short with a badge embroidered on the front. Then he strapped on his gunbelt, checked to make sure that a round was chambered in his pistol, and walked to the dock. Belker whined from the back yard when he heard his master walk by, but Hall only called for him to hush as he passed. He took his boat out far enough into Skull Creek that he could see the causeway that led to Pinckney Island. After setting the brand new anchor against the current, he turned on his laptop to work on his monthly report. The weather was far too beautiful to be stuck inside, and when he was with Jimmy they had always done their paperwork outside unless it was too cold or wet. He picked this spot to do his work for two reasons: His presence would make boaters think twice about disregarding the posted 'no-wake' zone, and he would be able to watch the sun set over the water.

The laughing gulls mocked him as he added up the gallons of gas he had burned and the hours he had spent on the water. He noted that he had erected one osprey nesting platform and made a mental note to check and see if the new platform had attracted any nesting birds. He detailed his involvement in the search for a missing boater (Gale) and the number of commercial boardings he had made (4). He had written eight citations and made one arrest for carrying a concealed weapon and possession of alcohol by a minor. He did not mention the disposition of those charges.

The low droning sound of an outboard motor buzzed in his subconscious as he typed, but it wasn't until the sound of the motor changed pitch that he glanced up to look for the boat. It was farther away than it sounded, probably more than a quarter of a mile from him. Hall hadn't quite gotten used to the fact that sound carried so easily across water. When he spotted the boat his heartbeat increased and he grabbed his binoculars.

It was a camouflaged jon boat and it was speeding away from him. The wake from the boat showed that it had been headed toward him but had turned sharply away. The lone occupant all but confirmed his identity when he looked behind him to see if he had been noticed.

Hall quickly started the motor on his boat and pulled the anchor free from the muddy bottom. By the time he was under way the suspect was more than a half a mile away, but on the open water Hall was able to take full advantage of his more powerful boat engine. He trimmed the motor as high as it would go and kept the throttle wide open until tears formed in the corners of his eyes. The fleeing suspect knew the lawman had a faster boat and cut sharply across a shallow point. Hall had to take a longer route through deeper water but continued to close in on his quarry. There were no shallow creeks nearby, nowhere for the boat to disappear. Just after the smaller boat crossed underneath the highway bridge it swerved violently toward the shore where the tide had retreated and exposed a maze of oyster rakes jutting out of the mud.

When it ran out of water, the lightweight jon boat skidded across the sticky gray mud for ten yards before it slid to a stop. Even as the propeller chewed into the mud and shells, the driver leapt from the craft and started to run through the mire. He fell several times trying to reach his goal of firm ground that was a long way away.

The engine protested with a scream, and the boat shook and shuddered when Hall slammed his motor into full reverse to keep from grounding. He knew the suspect was as good as caught. There was nowhere for him to go once he reached the mainland. Hall hoped that a man covered from head to toe in marsh mud would be easy to spot. Just as he got on his radio to call the sheriff's department for assistance, he heard a terrifying noise above him on the bridge and he ducked to avoid whatever was coming.

The screech of skidding tires was capped off by the sound of metal slamming against metal and concrete. Thousands of tiny pieces of glass rained down onto him from the bridge, and he heard someone scream. Hall looked at his suspect, who had also stopped to see what had happened, then swung his boat away from the shore.

Hall immediately radioed for help and requested an ambulance. He tied his boat to one of the bridge supports and hoisted himself up onto a ladder that led up to the top of the bridge. Just as he reached the catwalk his foot slipped on a pile of seagull excrement and he found himself momentarily hanging on by only one hand, twenty feet above the water. He quickly regained his balance, climbed onto the catwalk, and jumped over to the roadway.

Hall saw a tractor-trailer rig on its side and on top of another car. Three other cars had slammed into each other behind the semi. Hall ran toward the wreckage and pushed his way past several other people who had gotten out of their cars to help. The air was thick with diesel fumes, and the concrete was slick with anti-freeze and gasoline. Even when he stood next to the car he could not tell what make it was. It was crushed beyond recognition and so was anyone who was inside.

There were other people hurt as well. Someone was helping the truck driver out of his cab, and a young woman was sitting behind the steering wheel of her station wagon with blood streaming out of a gash on her forehead. Two young men in jeans and t-shirts with telltale Marine Corps high-and-tight haircuts were attending to the bleeding passengers of yet another car.

"There's a first aid kit down on my boat," Hall told one of the Marines. He took notice of Hall's uniform and hopped onto the catwalk and disappeared down the ladder.

"Is anyone critical?" Hall asked the other Marine. His training was starting to kick in. He needed to identify the more severely injured victims for the paramedics when they arrived.

"No sir, not in this car," the young man answered. "Probably just a broken nose." Hall noticed the young man had a stainless steel clasp where his left hand should have been.

Hall nodded and checked the third car. The driver had been wearing his seatbelt and was not injured at all. Someone in a nurse's uniform was using Hall's first aid kit to help the woman with the bleeding forehead. Now he turned back to the car underneath the truck.

Just as he began to hear sirens approaching, a Coast Guard helicopter circled above him and then landed in the travel lane that had been blocked by the accident. Hall reasoned that they must have heard him call for help on the marine radio and he was glad to see two Coasties carrying medical packs jump out of the chopper and head toward him.

As the adrenaline in his veins began to subside he began to worry more and more about the crushed automobile. Even when the fire department arrived and began to place hydraulic jacks underneath the overturned truck, he knew that whoever was underneath it was dead.

As more of the car became visible, his heart grew heavier and heavier. Hall saw the body of a young woman in the wreckage. One of the jacks slipped and a portion of the truck slammed back onto the car and Hall watched it fall on her for a second time. His blood pressure dropped dramatically. Everything he heard had a hollow ring, and he felt just as he had in the seventh grade when he watched the doctor put some stitches in his brother's knee. He stumbled to the guardrail, squatted down, and put his head between his knees. In the stillness of the moment he thought he heard the surf pounding in his ears.

"Are you OK?" It was one of the Marines. He shook out a cigarette and offered one to Hall. "The nicotine will help you feel better."

Hall shook his head. Within a moment the color returned to his face and he stood back up.

"I'm alright." The Marine walked away without saying anything else.

The fire department lifted the truck off of the car and was beginning to cut apart the roof. Several deputies and state troopers were there taking statements from witnesses and keeping the onlookers back. Hall wished that someone would keep him away.

When the "jaws of life" stopped cutting, Hall watched the rescuers peel back the twisted sheet metal and motion for a paramedic. Hall watched the medic kneel down into the car and stand back up much too quickly. The medic shook his head slowly at the firefighter

Hall approached the car and heard a trooper calling for the county coroner on his radio. The medic who pronounced the victim took a white sheet off of his gurney and was getting ready to drape it over the victim when Hall grabbed his arm.

"Wait just a second," Hall said

Her face looked too peaceful. If he hadn't looked below her neck he would have thought that she was merely sleeping. But his eyes were drawn lower, where the enormous weight of the truck had crushed her torso and severed her legs from her body. The blood was so plentiful Hall could smell it in the air.

"Did you know her?' the medic asked him.

Hall answered so quietly that the man had to ask him again.

"Not really," Hall whispered. "But I saw her in court the other day."

After he gathered his first aid kit, he took one last look at the accident scene. All of the cops, the medics, and the firemen were busy treating the victims or cleaning up the debris. He realized he wasn't needed any longer. He climbed back down the ladder and into his boat, thankful beyond words to be leaving the scene of death. Before he could open his canteen of water his emotions overwhelmed him and he slumped into the helm seat and just sat there for a long time.

After taking a few minutes to compose himself and drink some water, Hall motored over to the marsh grass and nudged his bow into the mud. His brand new rubber boots paid for themselves when he took his first step out of the boat. The mud was so thick that it almost sucked off his boots with every step, and he had to use his arms to help pull his legs up every time he took a step.

When he reached the abandoned jon boat he tied a line to it and played out the rope as he walked back to his boat. He hopped onto the bow of his boat butt-first and scooted around the gunwale on his rear end until his feet reached the water and he could wash the mud off of his boots. Then he tied the line from the jon boat to the front of his own boat and shifted into reverse.

For a moment he thought that he would have to call for a salvage boat but once the small aluminum boat started moving he was able to drag it back to the water. He moved the line to the stern of his boat and then started for the municipal dock in Beaufort.

It didn't take long for him to realize that the trip to Beaufort towing the impounded boat would take over an hour since he had to travel at such a low speed. Hall didn't want to be on the water towing a boat after dark so he decided to take the impounded vessel to the public boat landing on Pinckney Island and call for a tow truck. He hoped a roll-back wrecker would be able to winch the flat-bottomed boat onto its bed and take it to the county impound lot.

Since the road was still blocked from the accident, it was dark when the wrecker finally arrived. The driver told Hall he had never tried to haul a boat before but as long as he wasn't responsible for the damages he was willing to try. Once he backed down the boat ramp to the water's edge and tilted down the truck bed, the jon boat went on without a hitch. The driver smiled at Hall as he strapped down the boat for transport and wondered out loud if this might be a new way for him to make some money. Hall gave him directions to the impound lot and then shoved off for Beaufort in his boat. He would be there quicker than the driver, who agreed to pick him up at the marina.

Chapter Twenty-Three

Hall wished he had worn a jacket for the boat ride to Beaufort. The water was flat and calm, and there was enough light from the newly risen and waxing gibbous moon for him to safely travel as fast as his boat could go. When he reached the town he tied up his boat at the city marina, and a few minutes later the wrecker driver pulled up and Hall rode with him to the impound lot. The parking lot was crowded with cars and trucks and a few old motorcycles. Most of them had been seized under the new DUI laws and were going to be auctioned off with the proceeds going to the school system. A few were abandoned cars that were towed in by the police and were so ramshackle that no one had shown up to claim them.

Hall helped the wrecker driver back into a vacant spot between a badly wrecked police car and a Camaro that was missing its wheels. The driver unchained the jon boat and gently slid the boat onto the ground. Hall was filling out an inventory sheet when a deputy pulled up and got out of her patrol car. She walked over to Hall and asked him where he found the stolen boat.

"A poacher jumped out of it next to the Highway 278 Bridge, across from Pinckney Island," he answered. He was so busy filling out his paperwork that he didn't realize what she had said.

"Is this your boat, Mr. Gallers?"

Hall looked up from his writing to see who she was speaking to. An old man wearing a wrinkled face and a white, long sleeved dress shirt that was buttoned up to the top button under his overalls got out of the patrol car and walked with his cane over to the boat. There were no registration numbers on the boat and Hall hadn't found the serial number yet to run through records. He had a feeling that he didn't have to now.

"Yes ma'am that's my boat," the old man said. He spat a stream of bourbon colored tobacco juice onto the hood of the shoeless old Chevy.

This was not the man he chased a few hours ago. Hall knew what was next. He had a friend in college that had done the same thing after he had gotten drunk and wrecked his car one night.

"I sure do 'preciate you finding it for me Warden," the old man said to Hall.

Hall asked the deputy, "What time was the boat reported stolen?"

She too was beginning to understand what was happening.

"Mr. Gallers reported his boat missing at 1815 hours, according to the report."

Almost an hour after the poacher ditched it in the marsh.

"Say the feller who stole it got away, did ya?" the old man said with a smile.

"I don't think I mentioned that," Hall said. "I've found that things have a way of catching up with folks in the long run."

Hall walked away while the old man haggled with the wrecker driver over the fee for hauling his boat. He gave him some cash, and the driver winched the boat back onto this truck. The tow truck driver was beginning to think that the boat hauling business was going to be profitable after all.

From the crime report Hall learned that old Lazarus Gallers lived near Bolon Hall, a stones throw from Hazzard Creek where he had first chased the illegal netters. At least now he knew where to look for them the next time. He thanked the deputy for the information and walked back to the marina, letting the night air cool him off.

From the deck of his patrol boat Hall watched the driver unload the jon boat one more time. Together he and the old man slipped it off of the roll back truck bed and into the water. He waited until the tow truck was gone before he approached the old man.

"Better luck next time," the old man said. He was feeling brave now that the "real" law was nowhere around. "Them boat thieves can be mighty slippery."

"Is this your boat?" Hall asked. His serious tone made the old man look aggravated.

"You're damn straight it is," he answered.

Hall smiled and took his citation book out of his back pocket.

"You might as well turn that motor off Mr. Gallers. We're going to be here for a while."

Hall paid no attention to the old man's protests as he wrote him tickets for not having a fire extinguisher on board and not having a personal flotation device on his boat. The third citation charged him with not having a visual signaling device which was a requirement in coastal waters. By the time he was finished Hall had written up two-hundred and fifty dollars in fines and penalties.

The old man cursed him openly when he took his tickets and jerked the starter rope on his outboard.

"Where do you think you're going?' Hall asked. "You don't have the proper running lights to travel after sundown."

Lazarus shut his motor off and spit the plug of tobacco out of his mouth. He tied his boat to the dock and Hall helped him climb out of his boat.

"Some of us been's fishing 'round here before there were any regulations 'bout how to do it," he said.

"Is the fishing here as good now as it was when you were a kid?" Hall asked.

"Course it ain't. We used to catch spottails all day with just a white bucktail jig. Trout longer than your arm. Two or three crab pots would keep your freezer full and pay for your gas and oil. It ain't been like that since before you were born," the old man said.

Hall looked at the old man and nodded his head in agreement.

"I wish I could have been here then. How many bass you think there will be for my kids to catch if poachers keep netting them all?" Hall asked.

The old man grunted at the game warden and puttered down the dock with his cane keeping cadence. He shoved some fresh tobacco in his mouth and quietly muttered a promise to make his son in-law pay for the tickets and reimburse him for the money he had to pay the tow truck driver.

Hall waited a few more minutes before starting his own journey home. The tide was full now, and he could cut across the Parris Island spit without worry. When he was in Port Royal Sound proper he could see the red lights on the one hundred-foot radio tower that was on the mainland behind Pinckney Island. The tower stood so that when he left the Beaufort River it guided him right to the narrow channel that led to his dock. Exhausted, but like a good mariner, he checked and rechecked his lines and hosed down his boat before heading inside.

Chapter Twenty-Four

This evening seemed to be the coolest since she had been kidnapped. The sweat suit Arnold bought her kept her fairly warm but she still felt chilly. She had sores on her ankle from the handcuff and she craved a hot shower. Even when she had been aboard the hospital ship, where freshwater was rationed, she had been able to take a hot shower every day. She cleaned the wound on her ankle with some of the bottled water and a sanitary napkin from the supplies she had been given. The pain in her jaw was flaring up again, and she was afraid that her jaw had been knocked out of alignment. Every time she spoke or chewed her jaw made a disturbing popping sound and she'd had a headache ever since she had been knocked unconscious.

On the floor next to her bedroll were four small vertical lines she had scratched in the old wood. Tomorrow she would draw a horizontal slash across them, marking her fifth day of captivity. Arnold was yelling at the television for someone to buy a vowel and failing to decipher the simplest puzzle. He glanced over at her only occasionally and would always smile at her.

As Gale listened to Pat quiz his contestants she considered a question that she had forced herself to ignore. Why hadn't Arnold tried to force himself on her yet, if that was his intention? Gale had already decided that if that terrible moment ever came she would fight him with every ounce of strength she had. Was he telling her the truth when he said that he would let her go when he was finished with his job? Arnold had not tried to hurt her. Blondie had knocked her unconscious and thought she was dead. She had no illusions about him, but Arnold seemed different. She wondered if she could trust Arnold to keep his word. Would he let her go?

"Thanks for the clothes," she called across the building.

Arnold jumped up so quickly that he got caught up in his lawn chair and tripped and fell. Her body tensed with fear when she saw him move so fast.

"You're welcome," Arnold said as he stood back up.

She remembered a boy she had known in high school, a classmate who was so shy that he seldom ever spoke to anyone and never talked to her or any of the other girls. He was easily led and always hung around the troublemakers at school and was so anonymous she couldn't even remember his name, even though there were only thirty people in her graduating class. She wondered how much Arnold had in common with that fellow. Gale grabbed the edge of her blanket and pulled it around her shoulders. She needed to test her theory about Arnold.

"Are you from around here?" She knew from his accent that he wasn't a local boy but she had to start somewhere.

"No, uh, I'm from Pittsburgh, a neighborhood called Brushton," Arnold stammered.

"I've never been there. Is it nice?" Gale asked.

"It sucks. No jobs, a decent apartment costs an arm and a leg, and it snows too damn much. I ain't been back in twenty years," Arnold said. He dragged the lawn chair from in front of the television closer to where Gale was sitting on the floor. The sunlight outside was fading and the light from the television made shadows dance around the room.

"How did you ever get caught up with someone awful like your partner? You seem like a nice guy, but he scares me," Gale said and hoped she wasn't going too far.

"I've got to eat, just like you. Nobody is going to hire a felon on parole. I can't vote, I can't own a gun and I don't even have a high school diploma. I'm just trying to get by like everybody else."

Gale let the silence hang between them while she thought about what he said. He was right, she knew. Every job application she had ever seen asked about arrests and convictions, education and work experience. She didn't think it was fair for someone to have to pay for their mistakes forever.

"What about family? Don't you have anyone that could help you make a fresh start?"

Arnold shook his head, "I never met my father. I don't even know if my mom knows who he is. My grandma looked after me until she got tired of all my crap. The last time I got picked up as a juvenile nobody came to pick me up when I was released. I ran away from a group home, went back to our apartment, and everyone was gone. Nobody was there."

"How old were you?"

"Fourteen."

Gale thought about what her life was like when she was that age. She saw mountains for the first time in her life at fourteen when she went camping with her aunt and uncle. She babysat her young cousins for them and earned spending money for the arcade at the campground. She kissed a boy for the first time on that trip. Her grandfather had given her a little Sunfish sailboat for her fourteenth birthday and by the end of the summer she had a shelf full of racing trophies. Alone at fourteen was difficult for her to imagine.

"I'm sorry," she said.

Arnold shrugged his shoulders and took his lawn chair back to the television.

Chapter Twenty Five

Hall woke at five a.m., his usual time, and listened to the marine weather forecast on the VHF radio while he fried an egg and ate it out of the skillet. He took his morning cup of coffee to his kitchen table/work desk and started going through his mail. Belker was pleased to have some company, and Hall played with him for a bit while he drank his coffee. He guessed the pup was no more than three or four months old and was surprised by the young dog's instinctive urge to retrieve. He held Belker by his collar when he threw a tennis ball across the room and made the dog wait until he whispered 'get it'.

After a dozen tosses and retrievals the pup grew bored and was content to sit and gnaw on a plastic duck decoy Hall had given him. Hall began reading a fax that he had found earlier on the machine. It was from Cliff Anderson at the Waddell Center. The report was several pages long and would have been difficult for a layman to decipher. The clipped language and short sentences were not unlike criminal offense reports he'd read and written himself.

Hall resisted the impulse to skip ahead to the end of the report and read the conclusion. Instead he enjoyed digesting the results of the individual tests and hoped he would reach the same hypothesis. It had been a while since he had used his scientific knowledge and it was good exercise for his brain. The report didn't detail the actual testing procedures, but Hall knew what they were. During the last two years of college and in graduate school Hall had become familiar with the processes involved in determining the causes of vertebrate finfish mortality.

After a thorough physical examination, several individual scales were removed from each specimen. In addition, the otiliths or "earbones" of the fish were removed. These were used to determine the age of the fish, as it was necessary to differentiate whether juvenile or adult fish were affected. When Hall worked in the lab he had collected data for over a dozen on-going studies on everything from fish population levels to annual growth rate rankings to local water quality.

When a few scales and the otiliths were removed, the remainder of the carcass was ground into a pulp and submitted to a spectrometer for analysis. This machine provided the scientists with a highly detailed accounting of every element that was present and the amount of that element, no matter how small. The scientists checked the numbers on everything because even substances that occurred naturally in fish could prove lethal if too much were present.

But hydrocarbons were not naturally present in finfish. The level of hydrocarbons present in the fish that Hall had submitted showed a mean average of eight parts per million. Benzine and Naphthalene were the primary toxins detected.

Hall surmised that the fish kill was the result of a gasoline spill and Cliff made the same suggestion at the end of his report. It was not uncommon in urbanized coastal areas for small-scale fish kills to occur due to a gasoline or diesel spill. Hall knew for a fact it happened so frequently it was common practice for pleasure boaters to have an "ecological damage" rider on their insurance policies. Some marinas required the insurance before they would allow boaters to tie up for the night.

Hall put the fax down and referred to his notes from the day he collected the fish. He did not remember a slick being on the water, and his notes confirmed that. That meant the pollutant had been spilled quite some time before the fish had been discovered, or the wind and the tide had dispersed the slick.

At the end of the report was a handwritten note from his friend. He suggested that Hall return to the area where the fish were discovered and take bottom sediment samples. Another biologist at the center was conducting a study to determine how long hydrocarbon pollutants remained in the environment after a spill occurred. If significant hydrocarbon levels were present he would like for Hall, or someone, to collect sediment samples from the same area four times a year for as many years as possible.

Hall was thrilled to be able to mix some scientific research with his current duties. The request from Cliff was a small one, and Hall hoped it assured that he would be able to monitor the progress of the study. It couldn't hurt to keep his name in front of the staff at the Waddell Center. If they weren't hiring any biologists they might give him a good recommendation to someone who was. Hall wished Gale knew what he had discovered. She had been on the front line of the conservation effort in the Port Royal watershed and had done many things that had made a difference. Perhaps this study would lead to stricter penalties for polluters, or maybe scientists would discover a faster way to restore an area after a spill had occurred. She would have been pleased.

In his mail was a post card from Jimmy and Rebecca Barnwell. On the front was an aerial photograph of the massive naval shipyard at Norfolk. On the back Jimmy had written that their voyage had gone well so far, with the exception of a minor electrical problem that had kept them in Wilmington for a few days. He asked if there was any news, and Hall assumed he wondered if Gale's body was ever recovered. Tonight he would write a letter to his friend.

In the storage shed behind the caretaker's cottage Hall found the boxes he was looking for. The one he needed was on the bottom of the stack, and he remembered when he stored the boxes he had believed the items in this box were the least likely to be needed any time soon.

Inside were a small core-sampler and other dusty tools of a marine biologist. Some were well used from his fieldwork as a student and some were brand new, having been bought when his future seemed very certain. He grabbed a brand new lab book for his notes. If he was going to take scientific readings he might as well record them in the proper format.

He locked Belker inside the back yard. The pup managed a full-fledged bark for the first time, and Hall wasn't sure who was more surprised, him or the dog. The first fingers of the April sun were clearing the eastern horizon when he cast off from his dock, and when he passed Dawes Island he smelled smoke but could not see it. It had been over a week since any significant rainfall, and he was concerned. Jimmy had shown him areas that had been damaged by wildfires. Controlled burning was a valuable tool in wildlife management, but an uncontrolled marsh fire could be disastrous. Even after slowing the boat he could not tell where the smoke originated from, so he shut the engine down and drifted to a stop. Soon he was able to gauge the direction of the wind and slowly motored into the breeze. The smell of wood smoke grew stronger, but still he could not separate it from the morning fog and haze that had not yet burned off. Then he saw a wispy gray column of smoke rising into the sky.

The fire looked like it was coming from a group of trees several hundred yards back from the western bank of the Chechessee River. He saw a small creek that cut into the marsh and motored cautiously ahead, aware that the tide was quickly falling.

After idling along for more than fifteen minutes he came to a place that struck him as being unique for the lowcountry. On his left, the marsh suddenly gave way to solid ground that rose fifteen feet above the high water mark, which was unusual topography for this area. Where the marsh grass ended, palmettos, live oaks, and magnolia trees stood tall. Spanish moss draped heavily from the tree limbs. At the waterline was a small sandy beach, and on the sand was a small camouflaged jon boat.

Hall beached his boat, checked the jon boat closely and determined it was not the same vessel he had impounded yesterday. He knew he was not on refuge land but felt a duty to investigate the source of the smoke. He unconsciously adjusted his gunbelt across his hips. When the smell of bacon reached his nostrils he relaxed a bit, and when he found the campsite he was relieved. Four young teenagers were cooking over a small open fire, laughing and making a lot of noise. He called out before he got close to keep from surprising them.

The silence that followed confused him until he got close enough to speak. Every young eye was staring at his gun or badge. While his uniform didn't mean much to an illegal netter, he was glad to see it still meant something to these boys.

Surveying the camp, he was immediately impressed. Firewood was stacked neatly next to the tent, and the ground near the fire had been cleared of dry leaves and pine needles that might catch a stray spark. There were four separate piles of wood shavings and Hall guessed that last nights entertainment had been whittling, a time honored activity of young boys and old men.

They warmed up to him a bit after he complimented them on their camp and asked them if they were having a good time. When he told them how much he enjoyed camping out when he was scout, they offered him some bacon.

"Don't your parents worry about you out here all by yourselves?" Hall asked

The oldest boy went into the tent and came out carrying a small cellular phone.

"We live just a few miles up the river. If anything happened, my dad knows where our camp is." Hall learned that all the boys had grown up in the area and had fished and camped nearby ever since they were little kids.

The boys followed Hall back to his boat, and he obliged their request to show them some of his equipment including the shotgun which was kept in a locking rack under the console where it was protected from the elements. By now their shyness had vanished, and he spent fifteen minutes answering questions about what kind of gun he carried and what the Fish and Wildlife Service was. He invited them to visit him on Pinckney Island and when he pushed off of the beach they were getting ready to go crabbing in the creek.

The excitement he had about helping Cliff faded for a moment. It was replaced by the satisfaction that by simply doing his job he had helped ensure that the boys he just met, and generations after them, would be able to enjoy this wonderful ecosystem. Some of that pride was scraped off when he got stuck on a sandbar. He looked back and was thankful he was far enough away from the boys that they couldn't see him. Hall tried reversing off of the obstruction, but his propeller only churned mud. He was stuck until the tide rose again.

After sinking his brand new anchor into the marl his bow was embedded in, he pulled on his rubber boots, grabbed his binoculars, and walked to the bank. Within a few minutes he was on solid ground and underneath the shade of a spreading oak tree. From where he stood he could see the young campers splashing and playing at the water's edge—apparently the crabbing was a little slow. In the other direction he could see across Dawes Island to the Broad River and beyond to Port Royal Sound.

Through his binoculars he watched several shrimp trawlers head out of the sound and into the Atlantic Ocean. A single shrimp boat was coming in, and Hall didn't have to guess about the success or failure of their voyage. The boat rode low in the water, so great was her cargo. On the far side of the sound a rusty old barge was coming out of a creek near the Penn School. Hall didn't know there was a commercial dock in that area, but it didn't surprise him. He still felt geographically handicapped but learned more about his new home every day. Just a few minutes ago he had discovered a sandbar in the middle of an unnamed creek off of the Chechessee River and he would remember it the next time he traveled here.

Blurred movement caught his eye, and he refocused his binoculars on an oyster bar that had been exposed by the retreating water. A bird was walking among the knife-sharp shells and was picking up loose oysters in its bill. He watched with fascination as the bird flipped the mollusk into the air and watch it land against the other shells. After three throws, the oyster broke open and the bird dined on the half shell.

A large helicopter with two rotor blades interrupted his solitude, and he trained his binoculars skyward. The large rear cargo door was open, and two airmen seemed to be looking right at him. He could only imagine what the view must be like from up there. When he found the barge again it had barely moved and was struggling against the weakest part of the incoming tide. It seemed to give up and turned into another creek, not far from where it had started.

Chapter Twenty-Six

A rnold hid in the wheelhouse while Blondie stomped around the deck of the barge, cursing and swearing and making threats that Arnold was glad he could not hear. He was not wearing a life jacket and was terrified that Blondie might toss him overboard now that the hydraulic system was repaired.

This time it was the engine that was failing. The four-cylinder diesel was one cylinder down, and the slow rpm's made the miss in the engine seem like the boat was stuttering. Blondie insisted on overloading the barge with a second truckload of dirt and as a result they could not overcome the wind and the currents.

"Pull into that creek," Blondie said when he stuck his head in the doorway. Arnold acknowledged and turned the wheel.

He watched the depth finder closely, and it seemed the creek was deep enough for them to navigate. A trio of dolphins splashed off of the port bow, but no one aboard noticed. Both passengers had their eyes glued to the horizon, scanning the water for any other vessels or people that might detect what they were about to do. Other than the distant shrimp trawlers and a single sailboat near the horizon there were no other ships nearby.

"Go ahead," Blondie said.

Although Arnold had managed to repair the hydraulic system that operated the bottom opening mechanism of the barge he had to use the auxiliary controls which were located below decks. As soon as he threw the heavy lever he felt the boat shudder as she suddenly became several tons lighter.

Since he'd seen a bulldozer operator set himself on fire at the removal site in Beaufort, Blondie waited until the flammable soil was dumped before he lit a cigarette. Arnold was pleased that he seemed much calmer now.

"One more load," Blondie said.

Arnold grunted and nodded his head. He had a few things to accomplish himself before their partnership was dissolved.

In the wake of the decrepit barge, the contaminated soil drifted to the bottom, carried inland by the now rising tide. A lethal underwater cloud soon spread from the surface to the bottom of the creek and began to kill. Surprisingly, the first to die was not a fish, but a bird. A common loon had been swimming underwater, harassing a school of mullet, when it swam into the deadly mixture. The chemicals first began to burn the bird's eyes, panicking the creature and confusing it so that it swam deeper instead of towards the surface. The bird drowned before realizing its error.

Twenty thousand immature brown shrimp were the next to perish. A school of over two hundred juvenile redfish, which were feeding on the shrimp, died as well. The three dolphins sensed the danger immediately. Since they did not have gills, they were better able to withstand the poisoning. Instinct drove them from the creek to the safety of deeper water. The total number of casualties was impossible to count; Innumerable oysters, crabs, stingrays and clams would die over the next few days. Birds and other animals would eat the dead and dying and would poison themselves in the process. As the dolphins once again passed the boat that brought devastation to their home, the distinctive stuttering rhythm of the missing engine was etched in their brains as the sound of death. They fled at full speed, easily out-pacing the decrepit old boat and its cloud of death.

Freed by the rising tide, Hall sped across Port Royal Sound and found the creek where Gale had discovered the fish kill. Before he began to collect samples he locked his latitude and longitude into his GPS. He needed to make sure that subsequent samples were taken from the same area.

The water in the creek was shallow enough for him to use a core sampler attached to the end of a fifteen-foot long fiberglass pole. After plunging the sampler deep into the bottom, he withdrew it and used a small plunger to extract the sample into a glass jar. It was a messy job and by the time he had collected three samples the deck of his boat was covered with sand and sticky, gray mud. He labeled and secured the glass jars and then dipped a bucket over the side and dumped the water on the deck to wash it off.

When he left the creek and re-entered Port Royal Sound he thought it would be a good idea to obtain a few samples from a creek where there had not been a fish kill.

Cliff Anderson would be able to compare the samples to determine how many pollutants were already present in the environment. Hall turned into the next creek and had gone less than one-hundred yards when he saw the oil slick on the water.

The slick was huge and went from one shoreline of the creek to the other. Hall could smell something that reminded him of a telephone pole in the hot summer sun and it overpowered the sweet smell of the salty air. This spill was much larger than an accidental discharge from an overfilled fuel tank or from someone pumping out their bilge, as Hall knew some people did in the creeks and other out of the way places.

His next act was to report the spill to the Coast Guard. They received his report and dispatched a small boat with a spill-response team. Hall hoped they would be able to position the floating booms before the tide started to go out. He then took several more bottom samples and some samples of water at the surface, ten feet deep, and near the bottom.

It was not until he noticed the dead loon floating on the water that he realized he had forgotten to put on rubber gloves. After doing so, he recovered the bird and began to collect some of the dead seatrout and mullet, stopping after he had a dozen of each. Hundreds of immature fish of several species swam upside down and in circles as they died. His sadness and anger grew with every fish that floated to the surface, dead or slowly dying, and he wondered why anyone would do such a terrible thing.

After the Coasties arrived and successfully contained the spill, Hall realized this was the same creek he had seen the old barge enter when he was on the bluff on Dawes Island. He tried to remember what it looked like but the only thing he could remember was how slow it was. He tried to visualize what color it was and "rusty" was the only thought he had. He knew the boat had an open cargo bay and didn't know if a boat like that could carry liquid cargo. Maybe the captain was just flushing old fuel out of the tanks. He imagined the fuel tanks on a boat that large would have been enough to cause a spill like this.

Hall didn't mention the possible suspect vessel to the Coast Guard. They would assign a Marine Science Officer to investigate the case, and he wanted to do a little poking around on his own first. On his way home he pulled into the Lowcountry Seafood docks. Silas was cleaning some fish and feeding Gale's bird, much to the delight of his customers. By the look of things they had enjoyed a successful day of fishing. Hall waited until they left with their catch to approach the guide.

"Looks like you had a good day," Hall said.

Silas shielded his eyes against the setting sun and smiled when he recognized Hall. He took two bottles of water from his cooler and offered one to Hall who gratefully accepted it.

"The fishing was good today, but the clients always make the trip. The two guys I took out were residents from the Naval hospital and were just grateful to get away for the day. They'd both been in Beaufort for almost a year but had never been on the water before. We caught enough trout and spottails to feed 'em for a week. They already booked another trip next month," Silas said.

They talked about fishing and the upcoming tourist season, the weather, and each other's past. Hall learned Silas was a Parris Island alumnus. He had a fierce looking bulldog tattoo on his left forearm, but he was so darkly tanned that it was hard to see in the fading light.

"Four years," Silas answered when Hall asked him how long he had been in the Marines. "I always said that I'd sleep late when I got out and I get up earlier now than I ever did when I was in the Corps."

Silas seemed surprised to learn that Hall was actually a biologist by training and peppered him with questions about the growth cycles of fish, Pfsteria, and how the shrimp-baiting season affected local shrimp populations. Hall helped Silas hose down his skiff and it was dinner time by the time they were finished.

"Hungry?" Silas asked him.

"Starved." Hall didn't realize how hungry he was until the question had been put to him.

"Sometimes I keep one for myself."

Silas held up a beautiful spottail bass and in a few minutes had reduced it to some nice looking filets.

Lowcountry Seafood was closed for the day and Silas opened the door to Gale's office with a key. They walked through the office and up a set of steep and narrow stairs. The fishing guide pushed open another door and they were inside a small apartment loft.

Hall was drawn to the windows at the end of the room which were open to the cool sea breeze. The view across Skull Creek to Pinckney Island was magnificent- the mirror image of what Hall saw from his own home across the water. The rest of the loft was well kept and just as interesting. One wall was covered with pho- tographs; a snapshot collage of family members, a high school graduation picture of Gale. There was a picture of Silas with two other young Marines, all wearing their dress blues. On the bottom of the frame was a brass plaque with a date and

"Semper Fi" engraved on it.

"I thought Gale lived up here?" Hall asked.

"We kind of shared it. She split her time between here and mom and dad's. She stayed up here if she worked late and needed to get an early start the next day. She'd been staying here a lot more lately."

Hall had picked Gale up here when they went out together, and he wondered if she stayed here to be closer to Pinckney Island.

"Do you keep in touch with your buddies?" Hall asked, gesturing at the picture.

Silas looked up from the fish he was preparing.

"Some of them. Not those guys, though," he said.

Silas dipped one of the filets in a bowl of buttermilk and dredged it through some corn meal.

"Our embassy got hit. Neither of them made it."

Hall regretted his question and asked if there was anything he could do to help. Silas asked him to make a pitcher of lemonade, and Hall was grateful that it was instant. After five years of living on his own he was still lost in a kitchen. He would have starved in college if Domino's ever closed.

"I found another fish kill today," Hall said.

Silas looked up from the steaming cast iron skillet.

"It was near the one Gale discovered last week."

"I remember her talking about it," Silas said. He didn't seem upset by the mention of her name.

"It was a fuel spill. The slick was still on the water when I got there. I saw an old barge nearby not long before I found the spill."

Silas was putting some shrimp and the golden brown pieces of fish on a couple of paper plates.

"Do you think it was intentional?" he asked.

"I do. I think he was flushing out his fuel tanks," Hall answered.

Silas wasn't able to resist any longer and took a bite of fish before he replied.

"He could have been aground and dumped some fuel to float again," Silas said.

Hall considered that possibility as he chewed a huge shrimp.

"This is the best shrimp I've ever had," Hall said.

"I netted them in the channel that leads to your place on the island."

After resolving to buy a cast net and taking a bite of spottail bass that was just as good as the shrimp, he considered what Silas said.

"I guess if he was aground and dumped some fuel to float, it's not quite as bad as dumping it for no reason at all."

"Still wrong, but not as sinister, I suppose," Silas said.

The fish was gone too quickly, and Silas insisted Hall take some shrimp home. On the dock Silas asked him what the barge looked like.

"It was pretty far away, but it looked like the kind you would see working with a dredge. A small pilothouse at the stern, a lot of rust, maybe some blue paint."

They exchanged phone numbers, and Silas promised to call him if he saw the boat.

"I'll have my dad give the description to his crews," Silas said. "If that boat is still around, it won't take long to find it."

Full of hope and good food, Hall walked down the dock toward his patrol boat. Gale's skiff had been loaded on its trailer and was parked in the gravel lot next to her truck. Her boat was one of a kind, with Soundkeeper painted in bold black letters on both sides and green sea turtles, grey porpoises, and brown sea horses painted haphazardly on the bright yellow hull. The boat looked as happy and full of energy as Gale had been, and she frequently used it as a background when she was being interviewed by one of the local television stations.

Hall had never seen an outboard motor that ran on bio-diesel, but it didn't surprise him that Gale had one on her boat. She was committed to her cause, which he realized was his cause as well. He climbed up into her boat and sat behind the wheel and wondered what had happened to her. Agency regulations required him to wear a Personal Flotation Device every time he was on the water, but he'd never seen Gale wear one. Hall's PFD was small and stayed deflated until it came into contact with water which made it activate automatically. But it was still cumbersome and hot. He could not remember stopping a single boater since he'd been on the job who had been wearing a life jacket. He'd once heard that the majority of men who fell off boats and drowned did so when they were pissing off the side. It was easy for anyone to fall out of a moving boat and watch it motor away. A good swimmer could only tread water for a couple of hours.

He opened the compartment under the seat and found Gale's video camera in a plastic bag along with her notebook. He flipped open the screen, pushed the rewind button for a few seconds, and then hit play. Gale was narrating, explaining that the scene she was filming was at the Live Oaks development and that the developer was in violation of state and federal clean water laws yet again. You could hear the frustration and passion in her voice, a passion he knew was missing in his life.

For just a moment, she held the camera at arm's length and her face filled the screen while she spoke. She was a beautiful woman, and he was struck with a sense of personal loss for the first time. He wished that he'd had the opportunity to get to know her a lot better.

Her handwriting was neat and flowing in the journal, just like he knew it would be. The notes she took were precise and well written. He flipped through the pages and was surprised to see his name written in the margin of one of the pages, along with his phone number and a question mark. Maybe she didn't know what to think about the new refuge officer. She wasn't the only one.

He put the camera and journal into the plastic bag and left them in the boat. Then he went home, to Pinckney Island.

Chapter Twenty-Seven

S o often it was the arrogance and ego of a criminal that got him caught. As the senior detective, Varnum was tasked with several ongoing cases on which he reported directly to the sheriff. One of those cases was to perform random financial reviews of certain county employees. Deputy Sheriffs, purchasing agents, tax assessors, and county inspectors were all required to sign paperwork authorizing their employer to review their financial status at any time for any reason. Varnum wished the authorization extended to elected officials as well but he realized that would make too much sense.

The records he was reviewing belonged to an inspector who worked for the Department of Environmental Health. Varnum knew he inspected wells and tested samples of groundwater for contamination but wasn't sure what else the job entailed. An anonymous call had been received by the sheriff's voice mail, and the caller had stated this inspector had been accepting payoffs for several years and had been hiding the money in his wife's accounts in order to escape detection. Varnum guessed that the anonymous caller was either the person who was paying the bribe or someone who was jealous of the money. He'd learned through the years that greed and jealousy were much greater motivators than doing what was right for society. The court order Varnum took to the bank authorized him to review any accounts held by the inspector or accounts that he was named the beneficiary of.

Unless Harold Peterson had won the lottery or received an inheritance, something was not right. The house he lived in was modest and easily afforded by a civil servant, he drove a ten-year-old truck, but his wife had a new Prius. However, the boat payment that was automatically deducted from his wife's checking account was twice as big as their mortgage payment. The boat was a forty-two foot Nordic Tug, a cruising boat designed to look like a tug boat. When he found a picture of the boat on the internet he felt a bit of jealousy. It was a beautiful boat with as many cabins as he had bedrooms in his house. The galley featured granite counter tops and a Force Ten stove that cost more than a semester of college for his daughter. A quick search revealed that last year's model went for over half a million dollars and that didn't include the monthly dockage fees at a new marina. The numbers didn't add up.

With the help of a federal grant the county had computerized its records management two years ago. Varnum had the authority to log onto any system in the course of an official investigation and he entered the records management system of the Department of Environmental Health. Inspector Harold Peterson had one-hundred and eighty-three open permits, job sites where he was responsible for taking soil samples, submitting them to the state laboratory, and then granting the final building permit, which had to be issued before any construction started.

Varnum began to scroll through the permits in Peterson's file on his computer and just when his eyes couldn't take any more he saw a name that interested him: Mark Lancaster. Two months ago Peterson was assigned a case for a company called Palmetto Properties. Mark Lancaster was listed as principal developer and broker. Varnum recorded the address of the permit site in his notebook and printed several other pages before he logged off of the system and turned off his computer.

After that he went to the locker room where he changed out of his coat and tie and into a pair of khakis, worn docksiders and a faded polo shirt. He drove slowly past the marina twice before he parked far enough away from the dockmaster's office so no one could see his unmarked police car.

The marina was full of all types of boats from simple fishing skiffs to live-aboard trawlers and sailboats. The tide was low, and the gangway that led to the floating docks was angled sharply downward. In front of a few of the boats were mailboxes and potted plants, and Varnum guessed the people who owned them lived there all of the time, just like a floating apartment. Varnum liked the fact that all of them had a waterfront view and no grass to mow.

He found the Peterson's boat after strolling the docks for a while and wrote down the vessel registration number in his notebook. He was curious to see whose name it was in, because neither Peterson nor his wife had shown a boat registered to them when he checked their names in the database before he left his office. It looked brand new and just as expensive as he thought it would be. The brightwork was spotless, and all of the lines and canvas were new and unfaded. The large anchor that hung from the bowsprit looked like it had never been used. In the boat slip next to Peterson's trawler was a small daysailer with a color scheme that matched that of the Peterson's faux tug boat. Varnum wrote down that registration number as well.

After walking the docks for a while and trying to imagine what the people who owned these boats did for a living, he stopped by the office and chatted up the marina manager. He told her he had a forty-foot fishing boat he was going to bring up from Savannah and was looking for a marina in the area. She was attractive and her sales pitch was interesting and he learned that for just a bit less than his monthly house payment he could lease a boat slip. Included in the monthly dues were water and electricity, cable television, wi-fi internet service, and twenty-four hour access to the showers, restrooms, and laundromat that were located in the clubhouse. The marina sponsored parties on Labor Day, Independence Day, and Memorial Day. She told him she lived on a thirty-foot Hunter sailboat in the marina, and he noticed she wasn't wearing a wedding ring.

He took the packet of information from her, and she told him if he came by in his boat she would be happy to show him around the area on the water. He was about to ask her if he could reach her after business hours at the number listed on her business card when the telephone on her desk rang. By the time she was finished with her conversation he had lost his nerve and thanked her for her assistance before he left.

The cigarette tasted sour and was only halfway gone when he flicked the tobacco out of the paper and put the filter in his pants pocket. He looked at all of the boats in the marina and decided that he would be just as lonely in a million dollar yacht as he was in a thirty-year-old, three-bedroom, one and half bath tract home that needed paint and new carpet.

After stopping for a mega-sized cup of coffee, he found Mark Lancaster's proposed development. When he drove by he saw an old front-end loader, a bulldozer and a rusted dump truck sitting behind a chain link fence. The gate was closed and padlocked, and it didn't look like anyone was there. He parked one street over and walked behind the property. The fence enclosed the entire parcel, but it didn't take him very long to find a spot where a fallen pine tree had pushed a section down enough so he could easily hop over it.

It looked like every construction site before the actual building started that he'd ever seen. At the back of the property, near the spot he entered, it looked like someone had been using the bulldozer to level the land by skimming off the top few feet of soil. There were wooden stakes with multi-colored ribbons hanging off of them and a temporary power supply next to a small construction trailer. The wind shifted and he smelled something that reminded him of hot tar. Then he heard the jingle of the chain on the gate. There wasn't anything to hide behind, so he jumped behind a patch of weeds and proned out in the dust to keep from being seen.

From his hiding spot he saw a black Trans Am pull into the lot, and the driver got out with a passenger. Varnum was too far away to make a positive identification but he was pretty sure who the driver was. The two of them went into the construction trailer, one of whom he'd had breakfast with not long ago. Varnum wondered if she was trying to get her loan paid off ahead of time.

There weren't any windows in the back of the trailer, so he stood up and walked back to the low spot in the fence and returned to his car. He moved it and parked so he could see the gate through his binoculars and began to wait. An hour later a taxi pulled into the lot and tooted its horn. With the binoculars he was able to confirm his earlier suspicions and watched his informant get into the cab and drive away. After she left, he saw the driver of the Trans Am climb onto the loader and begin to scrape up dirt and load it into the old dump truck. Varnum wanted to follow it when it left, so he turned on the radio and listened to a baseball game to pass the time while he waited.

Two innings later his cell phone buzzed in his pocket and he answered it. The communications supervisor told him he was needed to respond to a report of a stabbing on the far end of the county. A man had caught his brother sleeping with his wife and beat him with a tricycle in the front yard of their mobile home. The victim was critical and the patrol sergeant had requested a detective at the scene. Varnum told the dispatcher that he was on the way and lit another cigarette as he drove away from the construction site.

Chapter Twenty-Eight

"Can I eat over there with you, so I can watch TV?" Gale asked. During the brief time Arnold and Blondie were gone Gale had decided to test her theory. She hoped she was prepared in case she was wrong.

Arnold unlocked the handcuff from her ankle and she rubbed the chafed skin. "Thanks," she said.

Her resolve to fight faded somewhat when she stood next to him and realized how enormous he really was. His odor nauseated her and reminded her it had been almost a week since she had bathed herself.

"I always watch Wheel of Fortune," Gale said even though she never did.

She was surprised at how easily she could lie when she had too. She didn't even own a television and there was only a radio for entertainment in the small apartment above her office. She hoped lying under these circumstances wasn't a sin.

They were eating takeout burgers Arnold had brought when he came back with the boat. She was grateful Blondie had left without coming inside the old warehouse.

"I'd buy a vowel," she thought out loud, hoping to stimulate some conversation.

Arnold grunted his agreement and made a terrible guess at what the unknown phrase was. Food fell out of his mouth when he spoke and he spilled his beer on his grimy shirt whenever he took a swallow.

Although she nibbled at her burger to make it last, it wasn't long before her food was gone. Things were going well, but she didn't want to go back to her shackle just yet. She hoped he would begin to doze off shortly, as she had watched him do almost every night about this time. She knew he never locked the door and she planned to make a break for it at the first opportunity.

She had decided her best way to escape was by water. Even as large and slow as he was, Arnold might be able to catch her on land where he had the advantage. He knew where the road led and how far it was to a telephone or safe haven.

In the water, she felt she had the upper hand. Navigating while she swam would be no different that when she floated in a boat, she reasoned. It would take him too long to ready his small boat for pursuit, and she could swim or wade in water that the boat would never be able to reach. She hoped the water was warm enough to avoid hypothermia, at least for several hours. She was ready to die trying if that was what it took.

"Would you like to take a shower?" Arnold suddenly asked.

Gale leaned away from him and fear rose in her throat, but she forced it back down.

"Yes, I would," she said. "But only if you promise to give me privacy."

The blush on his cheeks proved, she hoped, that he hadn't thought of anything else. He led her to the far corner of the warehouse where a garden hose she had not noticed before came down from the ceiling.

"There's a cistern on the roof that collects rain," he said.

While she stood there looking at the hose, Arnold took a piece of rope and tied it from one wall to another. Then he took one of the sheets from his lawn chair and rigged up a make shift shower curtain. After showing her how to make the water flow, he went back to his spot in front of the television.

Gale undid the hose and started the water but watched Arnold before stepping behind the sheet. Arnold didn't even glance her way, but still she did not trust him. She stripped to her bra and panties and stepped underneath the feeble stream of water in her underwear.

The water was warm from the sun which gave her hope that the marsh water would be too. There was an old piece of soap on the floor and after she felt like she had gotten any dirt off of it she lathered up her body and hair, quickly rinsing so she could keep her eyes open. Even when she spent months at sea on the hospital ship she had never gone this long without bathing. More importantly her spirit felt renewed as well. If she could have shaved her legs, she would have almost felt normal.

After she stopped the flow of water by crimping the hose with a piece of wire she listened to the water dripping through the floor and into the mud below the building. It was low tide. She had known that instinctively, just like a creature of the sea, but the dripping water confirmed what she already knew.

She knew the tide would be full again at one o'clock in the morning, six hours from now, and it also told her she had been a prisoner for six days. Over one hundred and forty hours, and she remembered every second of every hour. Gale knew she could swim to freedom if she got the opportunity and she was determined to be ready when the chance presented itself.

There was no towel for her to dry off with, so she stood and let herself drip dry. She thought about using the shower sheet to dry off with but couldn't bring herself to touch Arnold's bed linens. Only after she had been quiet for several minutes did Arnold turn her way, and then only after asking if it was all right.

"Are you done?" he asked.

"Yes," she said, walking toward him. She was wearing the clean sweat shirt and warm up pants he had brought her.

Now that she was clean she realized how terribly pungent her captor was. She hadn't seen him use the shower since she had been there and had no idea how long it had been before that since he'd bathed. She didn't want to know.

"That was very nice of you. Thanks."

Arnold seemed to enjoy the compliment.

They watched the end of Jeopardy!, and Gale saw his eyes begin to droop. Out of the corner of her eye she watched his eyelids dance until they were closed. Her heart raced and she worked to breathe as shallowly as possible to keep from making too much noise.

How much of a head start did she need? She decided if she could make it to the door before he reacted, she could make it to the water. Through the window she could see that the sky was clear. As soon as she was away from Arnold she would be able to orient herself by the stars. She knew exactly where Ursa Minor would be in late April and she felt certain the glow from the lights in Beaufort or Hilton Head would be visible as well. If she made it to open water, the tide and currents would direct her. She knew she could escape if she could just get to the water.

Each time Arnold's chest rose and fell Gale considered herself one breath closer to freedom. By her watch, Arnold had not opened his eyes for eight minutes. His breathing was heavy and regular, and his chin rested on the folds of fat of his neck. Somehow he was able to keep from spilling the beer that was balanced on his belly.

Her eyes darted from him to the door and back. Her pulse was racing and she was ready. She briefly considered trying to sneak to the door before she began to run but was afraid he would stir as soon as she moved. Like an Olympic sprinter, she had to reach her maximum velocity within her first few steps. She closed her eyes and said a quick but sincere prayer.

The loud crack of thunder startled her and she and Arnold rose from their chairs at the same time. They were both wide-eyed and staring at each other. Arnold looked like he was trying to figure out where he was and what was going on. He'd slept in so many different places it always took him a few minutes to get his bearings.

"That storm sure is getting close," she said.

Arnold nodded tentatively and opened his mouth as if he was trying to talk.

"Uh-huh," was the best he could do on such short notice.

Gale said she had to use the bathroom and walked out of the blue light from the television. Arnold struck his forehead with his fist so hard that it made an audible "whack".

"How stupid can I be?" he asked himself when she was out of earshot. When he wasn't with her, he could think of so many things to say to her. He wanted to start off with an apology to make sure she knew that none of this was his idea. If he wanted her to like him, he had to show her he and Blondie were nothing alike.

Arnold owed Blondie almost ten thousand dollars from gambling with him and when Blondie offered to forgive his debt and pay him for a few weeks work, he jumped at the chance. He had no idea that they were going to dump toxic dirt into the sea, but even when he found out he didn't care. Like most people Arnold saw only the vast expanse of water and salt marsh and assumed Mother Nature could handle anything that man threw at her. He needed the money.

Not long into the deal he saw his partner threaten the real estate developer with his switchblade and realized his partner was capable of really bad things. Arnold didn't care what his partner did and didn't feel sorry for anyone who got involved with Blondie. He just didn't want to go back to prison. He wouldn't, couldn't go back. Then his partner had murdered someone, at least Blondie believed that he had. And now Arnold found himself right in the middle of it, bound to Blondie with Gale's blood. He knew he had to keep Gale a secret, but that was only half of the battle. He wanted her to like him.

Standing with his fists clenched and beads of sweat pimpling out on his forehead, he worked up the nerve to apologize. He wanted to ask her forgiveness and ask her if they could be friends. That was the first step. He hadn't spoken like this to a girl since the seventh grade when that awful Fatima had laughed at him for trying to hold her hand on the school bus. He'd never been with a woman he hadn't had to pay for. If he could get away from Blondie and make Gale like him, he thought he could change his life around. With someone to help him he could find a decent job and start over. Gale represented the best opportunity he'd had in a long, long time.

Gale came out from behind the bedsheet, where the hole in the floor was, and walked over to her bedroll without looking at Arnold. She hoped if she didn't make a big deal about being chained up again, he wouldn't either. Maybe he'd even forget.

But a few minutes after she had been lying there, she heard the chain and handcuffs jingle when he picked them up. She stuck her leg out of the blanket and he stared at it for a moment before he fastened the cold steel around her ankle once again. Her best opportunity was gone. She told herself not to, but couldn't help it. She cried herself to sleep one more time.

Chapter Twenty-Nine

The spring pollen was settled by the previous evening's storm, and the warm breeze promised an even warmer afternoon. It was just light enough to see the road when Hall hopped on his mountain bike and rode the three miles to the visitor parking lot as fast as he could in the highest gear. He rested in the parking lot and drained his water bottle when the first visitors to the refuge arrived and parked their cars. A young couple with children unloaded picnic baskets and daypacks, and a serious birdwatcher started down one of the trails with a telephoto lens so large it dwarfed the camera it was attached to. He enjoyed watching everyone with anonymity for a few minutes then sprinted back to his cottage on the bike, feeling the burn in his thighs.

After eating breakfast, he wrote a letter to Jimmy Barnwell, telling him about the fish kills and getting the boat stuck. He thought Jimmy would be glad to hear he hadn't sunk it yet. There was much more he wanted to talk with Jimmy about—the wreck on the bridge, his first taste of the criminal justice system, and the fish kills, Gale. Depressing things he didn't want to put into a letter.

After studying his navigational charts for over an hour, Hall believed he had a good idea where the barge would be if it was still in the area. If the skipper had fuel problems, the boat would most likely be docked at one of the commercial docks along the waterfront in Beaufort.

Belker chased a tennis ball Hall threw for him until he saw the squirrel. The two creatures stared at one another until the squirrel's prey instinct kicked in and Belker assumed his role as predator. Hall joined the pursuit, not wanting anyone to know he was guilty of violating the strict "No Dogs" policy for refuge visitors.

He had convinced himself that being a resident and not a visitor excused him from that particular rule. He found Belker at the foot of a sweet gum tree where the squirrel was perched safely out of harm's way.

Hall put the pup in the back yard and got dressed for work. He pulled the wide elastic straps of his body armor tight against his torso and knew it would be soaked through with sweat before the day was through. The brown, polyester uniform shorts were ugly as sin, but he was more interested in comfort than style and put them on instead of his trousers. He threaded his handcuffs, extra magazines, and holster onto his belt and when he put the .40 Glock in the holster he was twelve pounds heavier than he was in his boxers.

After checking the oil in his boat motor, Hall took the shotgun out of its locking rack under the console and confirmed it was loaded, replaced it, and motored into Skull Creek. Hall knew a lot of recreational boaters and fishermen would be out on a Saturday, so he swung south around the tip of the island and back up Mackay Creek to the public boat ramp.

The parking area was full of trucks and cars with empty boat trailers parked in the gravel lot. A couple was trying to launch a brand new bowrider, and their words grew heated as their frustration with the boat and trailer manifested into anger with one another. Finally the boat slipped into the water, and they were happy again.

A few people were fishing from the dock, and they made a half-hearted attempt to hide their breakfast beers when they saw the patrol boat. Hall pretended not to notice and waved. Two boats were anchored near the cement pilings of the highway bridge, the anglers were fishing for the sheepshead that were attracted to the barnacles and other marine life. He eased up to them and checked their fishing licenses. All the fishermen had a license, and each boat had the proper floatation devices, fire extinguishers, and signaling equipment. They said the fishing had been slow so far and had the empty coolers to prove it.

Just as he was untying from the second boat, a speedboat came under the causeway at full throttle, oblivious to the no-wake zone. The waves from the speeding boat slammed the fishermen against the bridge, and when Hall started his motor to go after the speedboat the fishermen cheered. The speedboat roared past the boat landing, infuriating the couple who just managed to get their new boat under way, and almost knocked the woman out of the boat with its huge wake. The rouge continued south into Calibogue Sound without slowing.

His patrol boat was equipped with blue strobe lights and a siren, but Hall knew it was futile to activate them. With any luck the operator didn't know he was being pursued, and Hall might catch up with him when he stopped. Hall had his boat at full speed, and the speedboat continued to pull away from him. The boat was nearly a mile in front of him when he heard the noise from its motors change pitch. The boat dropped off plane, and Hall saw it pull into the Harbour Town Marina.

The red and white lighthouse at the Harbour Town yacht basin was the most recognizable landmark on Hilton Head Island. It was built by the developers of Sea Pines resort to serve as a reference for cruising boaters and it was the backdrop for the eighteenth hole of their signature golf course. Tourists used it more than mariners, climbing the steps to enjoy the beautiful sunsets on Calibouge Sound and the view across the water to Daufuskie Island.

By the time Hall entered the yacht basin, the captain of the speeding boat had already secured his dock lines and was preparing to go ashore. Harbour Town was crowded with people. Shoppers, tourists, and golfers waiting for their tee time filled the restaurants and shops. The open-air ice cream stand was busy and so were the gas docks. Someone was parasailing above Calibouge Sound. Hall felt a thousand pairs of eyes on him as he idled up to the offender.

He was better prepared this time. After being humiliated in court, he knew what to expect from someone who could afford a boat like this.

"Sir, I need to see some identification and your vessel documentation, please."

The operator of the speedboat quickly handed over the information.

"Officer, do you mind my asking what I've done?" he asked.

Prepared for an attack, Hall was surprised by the man's respectful tone.

"You sped through a no-wake zone when you went under the causeway," Hall answered.

Hall stopped speaking and began writing the citation. Speeding tickets for boaters didn't carry the same weight as a ticket for motorists. When a cop wrote a speeding ticket it was the increase in insurance rates that kept the driver honest, at least for a little while. Only a few states required boaters to be licensed and South Carolina wasn't one of them. The fifty-dollar fine for the violation was less than the owner spent to fill his gas tanks for a day on the water.

The man accepted his ticket and asked Hall if he could pay the fine without going to court. Hall told him that he could, got back into his boat and prepared to leave, when the man spoke again.

"Officer, I'm sorry about that. I usually go around Pinckney Island on the other side. For what its worth, it won't happen again," he said.

Hall said, "It's worth a lot. Thanks for understanding."

Hall left the harbor without looking at anyone else. He felt bad for giving a ticket to someone who seemed to be a pretty nice guy. Especially when he knew there were more deserving people. He decided to go to Beaufort to search for the old barge he had seen yesterday.

Chapter Thirty

"Take it easy son. Let the drag work for you."

From his perch on the poling platform of his fishing skiff, Silas York offered the words of advice to the nine-year-old boy who was tied to a good redfish. The boy and his father were his charter for the day and they had already caught some nice fish. This one, however, was the best by far.

Just when the fish was close to the boat it made another sizzling run, pulling out thirty yards of line against the drag and bouncing the rod in the young boy's hands.

The father echoed Silas's advice, and soon the fish was at the side of the boat again, tired and ready to land. The guide netted the big fish head-first and dislodged the treble hook from its lower lip. After showing the boy how to hold it without hurting the fish, he handed him his trophy and took a few pictures for the happy father and son. Silas took a picture of them with his camera because he wanted to remember too. After taking the fish back he laid it on top of the cooler against the ruler that was molded into the plastic.

"Twenty-seven and one-half inches," Silas announced. "A half an inch longer and we'd have to let her go."

For the first time since he'd hooked the big fish, the young boy lost his smile. When Silas opened the cooler the boy spoke.

"Dad, do we have to keep it? We've got plenty of fish to eat," the boy said.

The father and the guide looked at each other and both were pleased.

"Of course not, son."

The boy's smile returned and Silas knelt over the edge of the boat to release the fish back into its world. Then he stopped.

"Would you like to do it?" Silas asked.

The boy cradled the fish in his hands and worked it back and forth in the water until it swam freely from his grasp. The young man stared at the water for a while, and Silas thought about the contrast between these people and clients that wanted him to keep fish that were smaller than the legal length or take more fish than the law allowed.

"That's a fine son you've got there," he told the father.

A few minutes later the Native Son was grounded on the point of Dawes Island where Silas knew the sea breeze always kept the mosquitoes and no-see-ums away. He built a small fire from a stash of driftwood he kept there and filleted two of the trout they had caught. They washed down the fish and some potato chips with some cold sodas, and everyone agreed it was the best meal they'd had in quite a while.

After lunch they explored a few creeks on the northern side of Port Royal Sound, riding the rising tide into the marsh grass. They caught a few more reds and trout and ran into a school of ladyfish that spent more time in the air than the water when they were hooked. No good to eat, the small acrobatic fish provided the best entertainment of the afternoon.

Just as the day was about to end, Silas looked across the marsh grass and saw something unusual. Tied up to an abandoned fishhouse on the creek that led to the Penn Center was some type of large boat. He polled his boat a few yards further and took a pair of binoculars from underneath the console.

The superstructure of the boat had been blue at one time but was now heavily streaked with rust. This was the barge Hall was looking for. Before Silas could think of anything else the father grunted and Silas heard the drag on his spinning reel begin to sing.

"Holy smokes, this is a lot bigger than anything I've hooked so far," the father said.

Silas agreed. The fish, still taking line, headed for deeper water, and Silas started the engine on the boat in order to follow it. He didn't want the fish to drag the fragile fishing line against the sharp oyster shells, and when the boat was in deeper water he turned the engine off. The fish was stronger than the one the boy had caught earlier, but the father was stronger than the son. Both speculated aloud about what was attached to the other end of the line. Silas felt he knew but didn't want to break the spell.

"Shark!" the boy yelled as soon as the ghost-gray outline was visible in the water.

"Is it a hammerhead?" the boy asked the guide.

"Bonnet-head shark," Silas answered. "See how his head protrudes from his body, but his eyes are still above his mouth?" Silas asked.

The two anglers studied the fish in the water and admired the way Silas removed the hook with the gaff, without causing harm to the fish or risking his fingers.

"Pretty good way to end the day," Silas said.

Both of the fishermen agreed.

Silas cleaned the fish for his clients as he always did and didn't neglect Gale's bird. It came swooping in from the marsh as soon as he tied up to the dock and didn't leave until it had devoured the remains of two trout. The boy seemed to enjoy throwing the fish carcasses to the bird almost as much as he enjoyed catching the fish.

"Thank-you for a wonderful day," the father said as he paid Silas and included a nice tip. "We'll see you next year."

Silas washed down his skiff and thought about how nice it would be when he had a collection of clients who returned year after year. A year or two of hard work, he reasoned, and he would have a business that actually paid for itself.

When the boat was clean he made a sandwich out of some cold boiled shrimp, French bread, and homemade mayonnaise. In Gale's office he found the phone number he was looking for and called his friend.

Chapter Thirty-One

H all didn't receive the voicemail from Silas until he was back at home and had washed his boat down. He'd spent the entire afternoon looking in all the wrong places. He'd found creeks that weren't on the navigational charts and couldn't find ones that were supposed to be there. He checked dozens of fishermen during his search and issued eight citations, but he didn't find the barge he was looking for.

Now he was home and he didn't feel like going back out on the water. Hall wasn't comfortable yet on the water after dark, especially somewhere he hadn't been before. Silas's message said that he saw the barge in a creek that led to the Penn Center which was one of the few areas he didn't check today. He changed out of his uniform and into a pair of jeans and a t-shirt and went out to his boat and turned on his GPS unit. He cycled through the menu and located the route he'd taken when he dropped the confiscated fish off at the Penn Center. He was able to determine the latitude and longitude of the area that Silas had described and entered the coordinates into a hand-held satellite receiver. He put the unit, which was not much bigger than a cell phone, in his pocket and got the keys to his work truck.

Even with guidance from millions of dollars of satellite technology, and a five dollar map from a convenience store, it took Hall longer than he expected to find the road he was looking for. He turned off the blacktop and onto a sandy road that didn't seem to get much traffic. All of the lights on the truck went out when he flipped a switch on his dashboard except for a pair of small lights mounted under his bumper that cast a dull beam of light just a few feet in front of the truck. Trees and brush towered over both sides of his truck and closed in on him. Five minutes later the drainage ditch on one side of the road leveled out, and he pulled his truck twenty yards off of the road. The handheld GPS unit indicated it was less than half a mile to the water from here. He used a military surplus camouflage parachute to cover his truck, a trick he'd learned from Jimmy when they had conducted a fruitless stake-out for deer poachers one lonely light.

Back on the road on foot he held his flashlight parallel to the ground just a few inches from the dusty surface. There were several sets of tire tracks, but eventually he was able to determine that a heavy truck with dual rear wheels had driven up and down this road several times since the last rain. Hall turned off his flashlight, waited for his eyes to adjust to the darkness, and started walking.

A symphony of cicadas and tree crickets, katydids, and a tree frog seemed as loud as a rowdy crowd at a baseball game. A junebug buzzed past him and he was listening so intently to the concert that it took him a moment to notice ahead of him was a patch of night that seemed darker than everything else, like a black hole. He slowed his pace but his heartbeat increased. He felt the trees give way to open space and saw stars above him. He froze when he heard someone talking.

The faded wood exterior of the aging building blended into the surrounding darkness, and the flickering glow from a television was the first thing he saw. Instinctively, he ducked behind a bush. After watching for a while, he was satisfied no one was watching from the single window he saw. He forced himself to watch for a few minutes longer and just as he was ready to move again, a shadow moved across a window.

Now that he knew for certain that someone was inside Hall changed his strategy. He walked to his right through an open field and along the edge of the water, hoping that by taking the least expected approach he was less likely to be spotted. He walked like he did when he was still hunting through the woods; toe-heel, pause, toe-heel, pause. The wet mud along the edge of the water allowed him to progress without making a sound, and when he was still a good distance from the building he could tell there was a game show on the television.

Closer to the building he smelled chemicals and saw the silhouette of the barge. It was larger than he first suspected and listed just a bit to starboard. Even in this poor light he could tell how dilapidated it was. He did not believe it could be seaworthy. Headlights swept across the marsh, and he was silhouetted against the blackness. He heard someone yell inside the building and sprinted to the old dock.

"He's here!" Arnold yelled. The fear in his voice was evident.

He and Gale had been watching Jeopardy! together for the second evening in a row. Gale was waiting for her chance to escape, and Arnold was beginning to wonder if his partner was coming back at all. He was supposed to have arrived with the final load of contaminated soil yesterday, and when there was no contact for two days in a row Arnold was hoping their partnership had already been dissolved. He was beginning to believe that his guest was warming up to him.

"Get in the closet," he hissed at Gale.

She went into her familiar hiding place, and he rushed around the room trying to hide any signs of her existence. Gale heard a car door slam and Blondie yell.

"Arnold! Get out here!"

Fearfully he went outside.

"I think I saw someone."

Arnold looked around shrugging his shoulders.

"They were out by the boat. Get a flashlight, you idiot!"

Hall felt a sharp oyster shell cutting into his leg as he squatted beside the dock. The smell of creosote on the pilings was so strong it burned his eyes, and any hope he had of not being seen vanished when he heard the conversation between the two men. He knew there were at least three because he had heard two voices coming from the building. He dropped to his belly and slithered across the mud.

"Shine it over there."

Arnold obeyed and played the light across the ground. Raised in the city, neither man was going to trek through the marsh grass and muck during the day, much less at night.

"Go closer to the water." Blondie ordered.

The yellow beam of light danced over the dock, the boat and the marsh. Arnold moved closer to the edge of the marsh and was thankful he had put on his rubber boots when he got the flashlight for he was certain Blondie would have made him chase the ghost in his bare feet. No matter what Blondie said, he was staying away from the black and scary water.

In his hiding place under the dock Hall was directly below the man who was giving the orders. He could see the beam of light where the other man was stumbling around and was convinced that he was using the flashlight to see where he was going, not to look for him. He kept one hand on the pistol that was underneath his shirt. Mosquitoes buzzed in his nose and ears, and he tried to shoo them away with his other hand, but they were determined and he was outnumbered. The mosquitoes were equal opportunity pests and began to feast on the hunters as well. Hall could hear them slapping and cursing the critters that fed on them without mercy. He checked the positions of his pursuers. One was still above him on the dock, and the other was making a lot of noise moving through the spartina grass. Hall began sliding toward the water when something exploded at his left foot.

The marsh hen didn't surrender her roost without first loudly voicing her displeasure. The man on the dock almost fell into the water, and the other yelled and ran until he was on solid ground. Hall lay perfectly still and listened to his heart pounding in his chest.

"Get out from under there, or I'll shoot through the dock."

Hall knew it was a bluff. The man was guessing he was there because the bird flushed and gave away his position. He decided to stay put.

"I'm only going to count to five."

He was walking back along the old wooden planking and was directly above Hall when he took his switchblade out and flicked it open. The blade of the knife locking into position sounded just like a gun being cocked. Hall changed his mind.

"All right. I'm coming out."

Hall's first instinct was to identify himself as a federal officer and detain the three suspects while he called for assistance from the sheriff's office. But what would he do after that? The barge was high in the water which meant it was empty. He had no evidence these were the polluters even though he was sure they were. If they found out he was a cop they would leave before he had enough evidence to charge them. He would have to explain why he was sneaking around private property at night, out of uniform. He had made some mistakes already and didn't want to add to them.

Two men were standing beside each other on the dock when Hall crawled out from underneath it. The one with the flashlight was short and wide and the other one was tall and had hair so blonde it looked white in the darkness.

"Get up here," the blonde one ordered.

Hall did as he was told and noted that no one had told him to keep his hands up. He took this as a good sign. He also kept looking at the ground to keep the light from blinding him and stumbled on purpose. When he stepped onto the dock he was facing the two men and looking at the barge at the end of the dock. He did not see the third suspect he had heard earlier.

"What the hell are you doing here?" the one without the light asked.

Hall shrugged his shoulders and swayed back and forth. He kept his right hand hooked in a belt loop of his jeans, touching the butt of his pistol. No one had mentioned anything about calling the police. Most folks would call the police if they caught someone sneaking around their place at night, unless they didn't want the police around.

"He's drunk," the shorter man said.

"Shut up. Shine the light on him, not me, you idiot," the other man ordered. He acted like he was in charge.

In the split second the light wavered Hall saw the man who had threatened to shoot him had a knife in his hand, not a gun. He wasn't going to wait and see what he was going to do with it.

Hall lunged forward with his outstretched arm and stiff-armed the man with the flashlight off of the dock and heard him scream when he splashed into the water. He tried to run past the other man, but his muddy boots betrayed him and he slipped and went down hard on the rough wooden planks. Hall felt a kick thud into the back of his head and he saw stars dance in his peripheral vision. Before he could get back on his feet another kick slammed into his lower back, and pain shot down his legs. Again, in his kidneys, and it hurt like hell. Another lick in the same place and he grunted with pain. The man cursed him with a new word every time he landed a blow. Hall finally managed to scramble away, stand up, and hold up his hands to defend himself.

He blocked one fist, but the other slammed into his jaw and Hall tasted blood in his mouth and his teeth slammed together. The man in the water was still screaming and splashing beside the dock. Hall covered his face with his arms and they took the brunt of the next two blows. He saw an opening, shot his fist straight out and didn't know if the sound of popping tissue came from his hand or the man's nose. He didn't get his hand back up in front of his face quick enough and took another hit above his right eye. Blood started to trickle into his eye and he saw a flash of sliver in one of the man's hands.

Hall pulled his gun out and pointed it at the blonde head when the man stepped toward him with the knife outstretched. Neither man moved except for the heaving of their chests. The blonde man didn't drop the knife and Hall didn't tell him to. He wanted to shoot him right between the eyes and knew he wouldn't miss from three feet away, but he knew he couldn't. He had to call this in, to get some back-up here. It was time to answer for the mistake he'd made for coming here by himself before he made a mistake that could never be corrected. Before Hall could decide what to do next, the blonde man jumped off the dock into the water.

Hall ran off the dock and past the darkened building where the light from a television still flickered in the window. He felt the cool breeze on his stomach and glanced down at his shirt to see that it had been sliced from his navel to his sternum. Too many close calls for one night.

Chapter Thirty-Two

That night was the longest of Gale's imprisonment. Just after Blondie had arrived she heard some type of fight outside but couldn't tell what was going on. At one point she mustered enough courage to look out of one of the windows and thought she saw someone running away in the shadows but couldn't be sure of anything in the dark night. It scared her the most when the two men came back inside the warehouse.

"You idiot!" Blondie said. Gale heard several dull thumps and realized that Blondie was beating Arnold.

"I'll throw your sorry ass in the water next time, and I'll make sure it will be over your head."

Silence followed, and Gale knelt on the dirty floor and looked under the door. Arnold was sitting on his lawn chair, and it looked like blood was dripping from his nose. Blondie was standing over him rubbing his forehead above his right eye. Both men were soaking wet and dripping water on the floor.

"Take the flashlight outside and find my knife," Blondie said.

Arnold obeyed without any comment and walked out the door with his head hanging low. While Arnold was outside Blondie took a glass pipe out of his pocket and after he fiddled with something for a moment, held a lighter underneath it and inhaled deeply. Gale didn't smell the sweet odor of marijuana and wondered if he was smoking crack or meth, but knew it didn't really matter. She'd never seen Arnold do anything other than drink beer since she had been with him.

It was cool in the closet without a blanket, but she fell asleep curled up in a ball on the dirty floor with her head resting on one of her arms. The sound of a car engine woke her several hours later, and Arnold opened the closet door. He said nothing and led her to the chain.

"Are you all right?' Gale asked him.

She could see that his upper lip was swollen, and he had a cut under his left eye. He was still wet and shivering.

"Yeah. I fell in the water."

"Did he hit you?" Gale asked.

"That was a lot worse than getting hit."

Gale gave him a puzzled look.

"I can't swim."

Gale didn't say anything until after Arnold put the handcuff on her ankle and walked back to his chair and sat down.

"I can teach you," Gale said.

"Yeah, OK."

Maybe that was her way out.

The next time she woke up, sun was streaming in through the window and Arnold was gone. She ate one of the granola bars he had given her, drank some bottled water and stretched before she started her yoga. Today was the day, she told herself. She would escape today. She added another mark to the six other scratches on the floor.

Chapter Thirty-Three

Sunday afternoon, on his way home from church, Varnum drove past the construction site. The dump truck was now loaded with dirt, and no one was around. The black Trans Am was gone, and the gate was chained up. He decided to see if his suspect was at his mother's house before heading home. No one was there waiting on him, so he wasn't in any hurry to get there.

When he got to the house, the Trans Am wasn't there, but a navy blue pick up truck with government tags was parked in front of it. Varnum pulled up beside it and rolled his window down. A young looking guy with a swollen lip and short blonde hair looked down at him from the cab.

"What's going on?" Varnum asked.

The driver took off his sunglasses and had white lines where the frames of the glasses had blocked the sun's rays. One of his eyes was purple and blue. He gave Varnum a look that Varnum was used to giving, not receiving.

"Varnum, Beaufort Sheriff's Office," Varnum said when he held up his identification for the young man to see.

"Oh, yes sir," he said. Varnum was pretty sure that the kid was showing respect for his age, not his position.

"I've got an interest in this house. What agency are you with?"

"U.S. Fish and Wildlife Service. I'm refuge officer Hall McCormick. I'm looking for the driver of a black Trans Am."

Varnum told the wildlife officer to follow him, and they drove to the same diner where Varnum had eaten breakfast with a stripper not long ago.

"What kind of case are you working?" Varnum asked after he ordered coffee and the young officer asked for a soda.

"Illegal dumping. I think the guy who drives that Trans Am is connected to a barge that is responsible for dumping chemicals in the sound."

Varnum listened as Hall told him about the fish kills, and it was apparent how much the case meant to the young officer. He told him how he had collected the dead fish and discovered what chemicals were dumped and killed the fish. Last night the Trans Am was parked at an abandoned fish house where the barge was moored, and he'd had an encounter with the suspect. Varnum just listened, thankful that this Fed was unlike the others he'd worked with. In his experience they usually wanted all the information from local officers but weren't willing to share the details of their own investigation. He was a little surprised when Hall told him about getting into a fight with the suspect.

"He did that to you, the guy who drives the Trans Am?" Varnum asked. In the diner the black eye and split lip looked worse than they had earlier.

"Yeah, all this and a few lumps and bumps you can't see."

"How long have you been an officer?" Varnum asked. He couldn't believe any lawman would tolerate getting beat up without calling the cavalry and going back to even the score.

"Not quite a year," Hall answered. Varnum could tell that he'd hurt the young man's feelings by asking and changed the subject.

"The chemicals you found in the dead fish, could they come from some soil that had been contaminated by tar, like they use on railroad ties?"

"It's possible. Why?"

Varnum told him about the construction site where he'd seen the suspect loading dirt into a dump truck.

"We can get a warrant and see if the compounds in the soil match what I found in the fish," Hall said.

Varnum said, "We could do that, but there might be a better way."

Just a rookie, Varnum thought. He remembered when the job was as exciting to him as it was to the young man sitting across from him. Some days it seemed like a long, long time ago.

They made plans to meet the next day and go back to the old warehouse together. Varnum promised to email a picture of the suspect he was investigating, so they could be certain they were both looking for the same guy. Varnum thought he knew how to get a sample of the soil from the construction site without a warrant, and Hall said he would get it tested to see if the pollutants matched. Tomorrow was going to be a big day.

Chapter Thirty-four

In spite of being so excited about making good progress in the illegal dumping investigation and meeting someone who could help him with the case, Hall fell asleep on his couch not long after eating supper. He had tried to read a bulletin about caviar smuggling, but his eyes wouldn't stay open. He had been too jacked up and sore to get any sleep the night before and hadn't slept more than five hours in a row since he'd moved into the cottage. He never got a chance to catch up.

The telephone in his living room rang, but he slept right through it and didn't wake up until he heard his own voice on the answering machine telling the caller to leave a message. A citizen was complaining about someone who had tied his boat to the dock at the public boat ramp all day and it was still there now. It made it hard for other people to launch and retrieve their boats, and the caller suggested that if somebody didn't do something about it, he was going to pull the plug on the boat and let it sink. Hall checked another message he'd slept through entirely and found out another car had been burglarized in the visitor's parking lot.

Hall stood and stretched; thankful he let the machine take the call for him. He wasn't sure if he felt better than he had before his nap but hoped he had gotten a little closer to catching up on all the lost hours of sleep. He ate a peanut butter sandwich while he read his email and checked the long-range marine forecast. There was a cold front moving into the region from the southeast and a good chance of thunderstorms this afternoon, some of them severe.

He changed from his shorts into his uniform pants and went out on patrol in his boat. As soon as the sun slipped into the waters of Calibouge Sound, Hall took off the small, inflatable life jacket and put on a windbreaker that was also a personal flotation device. This was one of Jimmy's rules, and Hall thought it made a lot of sense. Just as most deadly car accidents occurred at night, most boating fatalities did too. The jacket had reflective tape sewn on the front and back, and Hall kept a small waterproof VHF radio in one of the pockets.

The Intracoastal Waterway ran along the entire eastern seaboard of the United States. It twisted around Beaufort and across Port Royal Sound and followed Skull Creek between Hilton Head and Pinckney Island. Situated between Savannah and Charleston, this part of the waterway saw a moderate volume of shipping traffic. Tugboats often pushed rafts of barges through the night, and yachts travelling north in the spring and south in the fall passed through Beaufort County.

Lights from houses along the water allowed Hall to navigate safely, but anything submerged in the water would be impossible to see. For safety's sake he kept the throttle just above idle speed and motored toward the boat ramp.

Since it had been a beautiful Saturday in April, Hall had heard the sound of power skis all day long. Because of this it took him a minute to realize he was hearing them again, but personal watercraft weren't designed to be operated after dark. They weren't equipped with navigation lights and were approved only for daytime use.

On the southwest edge of Pinckney Island was a small beach favored by jet-skiers. Teenagers mostly, they would launch their watercraft on the other side of the island and take coolers, chairs, and blankets to the beach. Then they would race around chasing each other and jumping waves. Complaints about littering and drinking were not uncommon. Hall was certain this was where the jet-ski he heard was operating.

He approached the area near the beach and could hear the distinctive whine of a small but powerful engine. When he felt he was close enough he turned on the bright spotlight mounted on the aluminum framed T-top on his boat.

There were two skis illuminated against the beach, and each had a passenger aboard. Hall immediately used his loudspeaker to advise them to come about and prepare to be boarded. One rider obeyed, and the other did not. He opened his water bike to full throttle and shot away from the flashing blue strobe light, leaving a rooster tail of water in his wake and his passenger holding on for dear life.

The obedient boater received a citation.

"I appreciate you obeying my orders," Hall explained, "but I can't ignore such a dangerous violation especially when you endangered the life of someone else at the same time."

He could tell the young man and his girlfriend were pissed off about getting the ticket but didn't verbalize their feelings. Hall escorted them around the island to the boat ramp so they wouldn't be a hazard to navigation in the dark. While he was there he noticed the boat that was supposed to have been docked there all day was gone.

"And don't think your friend got away with it. He's got to take his ski out of the water sometime," Hall said.

Hall was prepared to wait all night, if he had to. He could anchor far enough away from shore to avoid the mosquitoes while he waited. Someone that reckless was a danger to everyone on the water. When he anchored his boat and turned off the motor, he could hear the ski when the car traffic above him on the causeway subsided. It sounded like they were over by the beach again, zipping around in the dark. His boat wasn't fast enough to catch the speedy watercraft, and he decided he would wait until the owner began loading it onto the trailer. The cool evening breeze and the gentle rocking of his boat lulled him into a semi-conscious state, and his head began to bob up and down until his chin was resting on his chest.

The loud crashing sound of an air horn jolted Hall awake. He wondered what was making the sound when he realized the blasts were continuing in groups of three, the international distress signal.

He quickly pulled up his anchor, started his engine, and raced toward the sound of the horn. As soon as he cleared the end of the island he saw one of the ferryboats from Daufuskie Island in the middle of the channel. Every light on the boat was on, and several crewmembers were shining flashlights in the water behind the stern.

"Vessel in distress in Skull Creek, what is your emergency?" Hall asked over the VHF radio on the hailing frequency. He wanted to know how to approach if a passenger had fallen overboard and was in the water.

"Something ran into the back of us!" a voice on the radio replied.

Hall heard the Coast Guard radio operator try to raise the ferry boat again, but no one replied.

He switched on his blue strobe lights and shined the spotlight against the stern of the passenger ferry. The fifty-foot boat was constructed of steel, and Hall knew that the other party was probably on the losing end. He eased close enough to yell to a crewman.

"What happened?" he asked.

"Something slammed into the back of the boat," he yelled back.

Several of the passengers had gathered on the deck and one of them yelled to

Hall.

"I think it was a power-ski, officer," one of them said.

Hall cursed and slammed his hand against the steering wheel of his boat. He remained stationary and swept the water with his searchlight. He looked at the back of the ferry boat near the waterline and saw only a slight smudge of yellow paint. Three-hundred pounds of plastic and fiberglass didn't make much of an impression on six tons of iron and steel.

The Coast Guard radio operator had taken control of the frequency. She was advising all stations that a rescue helicopter was en route and the Beaufort County Sheriff's Office was sending their boat as well. She put out an advisory for all vessels in the area cautioning them that subjects were in the water.

"There it is!" someone aboard the ferry shouted. Hall followed the flashlight beam and trained his more powerful light on the water. The object floating on the water was not immediately recognizable, but he knew what it had to be. Two men in a small fishing boat startled him as they pulled up alongside.

"What can we do to help?" one of them asked.

"Work toward the mouth of the sound. If they were wearing life jackets, they should be drifting that way. I'll be along as soon as I secure the wreckage," Hall said.

He knew the tide was falling without having to think about it. Before he secured a line to what was left of the jet-ski he dropped a weighted marker buoy into the water to fix the spot where he found the wreckage. He knew the state game warden who would investigate the accident would need to know exactly where it occurred.

The personal watercraft was mangled and shattered. Fuel was leaking from the gas tank, and the handlebars and seat were missing. Hall looped a line through an exposed portion of the engine and secured it to one of the towing eyes on the stern of his boat. He used his light to inspect the wreck one more time before he began towing and noticed blood and hair where the handlebars should have been.

When he reached the shore, a deputy sheriff who had arrived in his patrol car helped Hall drag the jet-ski onto the beach above the high tide line. Hall asked the deputy if he would go back out with him to look for the victims, and he said he would. Hall gave him a life jacket to wear, and they motored away from the shore. On the highway bridge above the accident scene, a fire truck had arrived and was illuminating the area with a bank of powerful flood lights. The ferryboat was anchored and had swung one-hundred and eighty degrees in the current.

The fishermen who volunteered to help were close to Pinckney Island so Hall decided to check on the other side of the waterway, closer to the marina and the Low Country Seafood docks.

The deputy spotted the victim first, and Hall knew by the tone of his voice they would not be rescuing anyone. Hall was thankful that he had someone aboard to help, someone who had done this kind of thing before. He had never touched a dead body. The deputy grabbed the life jacket the young woman was wearing and used his other hand to feel her neck for a pulse. After a moment he looked at Hall and shook his head.

Even with the two of them working together it was difficult to get her body onto the boat. Finally they got her over the gunwale, and she fell into the boat with a sickening thud. Blood and water began to collect on the deck.

"Do you have anything to cover her with?" the deputy asked.

Hall had a blue plastic tarp in a locker and they used it to cover her body. After the grim task was over, they began to search for the driver. Hall knew he had to be dead, too, and hoped someone else found him.

"She looked about the same age as my daughter," the deputy said, breaking the silence that had lasted more than thirty minutes. "I wonder if we're going to find the other one."

Hall couldn't think of anything to say and just shrugged his shoulders in the dark. The sheriff's boat was on the scene now and joined in the search. Hall told them he had one of the victims in his boat, and he was instructed to take the body to the dock at the boat ramp where the coroner would meet him.

While they were waiting for the coroner to arrive, the second body was found by the fishermen. The crew of the sheriff's boat recovered it from the water, and by the time they arrived at the boat ramp, Hall and the deputy had already unloaded their cargo.

A sergeant with the South Carolina Department of Natural Resources had arrived on the scene and had assumed responsibility for the investigation. Hall met him in the gravel parking lot of the boat ramp and gave him a statement, beginning with the first time he saw the victims, hours ago when they ran from him.

After he was finished, the sergeant asked him if he would help out by trying to identify the victims. Hall agreed. He walked through the woods to the beach where he had left the jet-ski and copied the registration number in his notebook. He was walking back across the parking lot to report what he had found, when he noticed a car parked in the lot with a small empty trailer attached to it. The darkness hid the color from him but as he got closer he could tell it was bright red. He radioed in the tag to the dispatcher and confirmed what he already knew. The last time he'd seen this car the driver had been leaving the courthouse, flipping him the bird.

The coroner's van was just about to pull away when Hall stopped him and asked to see the male victim.

"I think I can ID him," Hall said.

The coroner stayed in the van while his assistant got out and opened the rear doors. He climbed into the back and pulled the sheet away from the young man's face so Hall could see him. Even in death the body reeked of alcohol. He took his copy of the dead man's arrest sheet from his clipboard and gave it to the state wildlife sergeant.

"Can you send me a copy of your report when you're finished?" Hall asked. The sergeant said he would. Hall knew a judge and an attorney he was going to send it to.

Hall stayed at the scene of the accident until daybreak. A news crew from Charleston was in the parking lot, and the reporter tried to get Hall to talk to her. She was attractive and made him feel important when she flirted with him but he referred her to the investigating sergeant.

Instead of going through Skull Creek, Hall took the long way home around the back of Pinckney Island. He didn't care to see the ferry boat or what was left of the jet ski again. He absently tied his boat to the dock and walked up to the house, let Belker out, and pulled the water hose down to the dock. He didn't want to splash bleach on his uniform, so he took off his shirt and pants and started cleaning his boat in his boxers and rubber boots.

He poured a healthy amount of bleach into a five-gallon bucket and diluted it with water. The long handled scrub brush kept him from having to get on his hands and knees, but the dried blood was difficult to remove from the non-skid surface of the deck. He knew it would hang around in other places for a long time.

The sun was above the trees by the time he was finished, and his body was covered with sweat. His face, neck, and his arms below his elbows were coppery brown, colored by the sun and the wind and the salt. The rest of his body was pale white and tired. He lay down on his back next to Belker on the dock and drifted off to sleep.

Chapter Thirty-Five

Arnold left without saying anything to Gale and was gone for several hours. He returned and found Gale sleeping, the same thing most prisoners did to pass the time.

"We've got to leave," Arnold said.

Gale was excited and scared, but she couldn't figure out what was going on. She wondered what had finally given Arnold the guts to leave Blondie.

"What about your partner?" she asked.

"It's his idea. He's worried about the guy who was snooping 'round here last night," Arnold said. She was disappointed to learn Arnold wasn't splitting from Blondie, but at least she knew what happened last night.

"Where are we going?" she asked.

Arnold didn't answer, and Gale decided not to ask any more questions.

Instead of taking the handcuff off of her ankle he used a pair of bolt cutters to cut the chain from the iron girder in the ceiling and it fell to the floor. She knew she could not swim away with the heavy chain shackled to her ankle, even if Arnold wasn't holding on to it.

"Get your stuff," he said without looking at her.

The chained dragged behind her while Gale grabbed her bedroll, sweat suit, and the bag of provisions Arnold had given to her. He led her outside where the sun was so bright it hurt her eyes. She looked around at the green marsh grass, the puffy white cumulous clouds, and the calm, dark water and realized she had never been indoors for so long in her entire life. This thought almost made her cry, but she was determined not to.

The old barge was at the end of the dock, and they climbed on board. The cargo bay was full of dirt, and Gale wondered how much poison the pair had already dumped into the sea. Arnold padlocked her chain to a pipe in the pilothouse and told her to sit on the floor. After he started the engine and went back to get his lawn chair and cooler, she stood up and peeked at her prison from the outside. She wanted to be able to identify where she had been held if she ever got a chance to tell anyone. It looked a lot smaller from the outside and like no one had been there in years. The fear of the unknown made her wish she wasn't going anywhere.

They cast off from the old rickety dock, and Gale heard a piling scrape the barge all the way down its side as Arnold tried to control the old boat. Gale made an educated guess that they were headed south based on the position of the sun and the shadows as they played across the boat. She knew they had entered a larger body of water when the boat began to rock with the swells. They had to be in Port Royal Sound, she deduced, but they were headed west and inland, not out to sea. She did not understand where they could be going. The Intracoastal Waterway ran closer to the ocean, up the river and north to Beaufort, south to Savannah. The rivers just got shallower and narrow the further upstream they went. Her dead reckoning was proved correct when she recognized the Broad River Bridge they were passing underneath.

A few minutes later Arnold slowed the barge and his frantic movements with the wheel and the throttle were rewarded by a solid bump against a dock that groaned in protest. Gale knew where she was. The only marina this close to the bridge was on Lemon Island, an old and small establishment that catered mostly to crabbers and their small boats and a few recreational fishermen. She remembered that every time she had passed by, the docks here were piled high with crab traps and marker buoys and there was always a lot of activity around the place.

"Don't move," Arnold told her after he tied the barge to the dock. Since she already knew where she was, she didn't want to risk his anger so she sat on the grimy floor of the boat and began to formulate a plan.

If she started screaming and yelling for help right now, she felt there was a good chance someone would hear her, but she couldn't be certain. Most commercial fishermen left the dock early and came back late, and since it was just after two in the afternoon, there was a chance no one was around. She didn't want to risk yelling for help until she knew someone would hear her. She could wait until she heard another boat approach, but then a sudden realization disrupted her thoughts.

Blondie was coming back. That meant that Arnold couldn't leave her on the boat.

Where would her next prison be?

Arnold came back on board before she had any time to consider the possibilities. He unlocked the chain from the pipe and looked around just like the bad guys always did in the movies. Then he told her to stand up and wrapped the other end of the chain around his hand.

He led her off of the boat and down the narrow dock where an old pick-up truck was parked. She looked for someone, anyone, but there was no one around and no other cars were in the parking lot. He made her get in the truck first and told her to sit down on the floor. Through a hole in the floorboard where the rust had eaten away the sheet metal she watched the road change from sand to pavement and back to sand again. When they stopped she checked her watch and knew they were fifteen minutes from the marina. A fifteen-minute drive meant she was between ten and twelve miles from Lemon Island, but she had no way of knowing which direction they had gone.

The mobile home he had driven to was surrounded by tall pine trees and was as rusty and decrepit as the old barge. She could not smell the marsh or the sea. An old car with no wheels was sitting in the sand in front of the trailer. Gale saw bullet holes in the side of the junked car. The sparse grass grew in scattered patches and was long and bent over, looking like a bad, green comb-over. There were no other houses in sight, and Arnold gripped her chain in his hand and made her slide out of the driver's door beside him. Then he took a key out of his pocket to unlock the door to the trailer, but the doorknob had been broken off. He pushed open the door and reached in for a light switch.

Gale screamed when the light came on. Two people were sitting at the kitchen table. One was a skinny girl with big fake boobs and heavy make up. The other, a bleached-blonde, was holding a bottle of liquor in one hand and a switchblade in the other.

Chapter Thirty-Six

Hall woke from his nap at the time he would have normally gone to bed, and it felt like he may have gotten a little too much sun on his pale torso. He was starting to understand there was no longer such a thing as a normal schedule for him. After tidying the kitchen and sweeping the small den, he gave Belker a bath out on the back porch. He picked up the t-shirt he'd been wearing when he'd gotten into the fight and looked at the slash in it once again. The knife had been razor sharp and would have slit his belly just as easily, he realized. He threw the shirt in the trash. At two a.m. he decided to catch up on his paperwork. The report detailing his assistance in the boating double-fatality was two pages long. He had to fill out a separate piece of paper for every day he worked, and this form was broken down into two-hour increments. Jimmy never complained about the paperwork and told Hall it was just part of the job, but Hall felt if he could be trusted with a gun and a badge, he shouldn't have to account for every waking moment of his life.

No matter how many times he had scrubbed his hands they still smelled like bleach, and he kept checking as he typed to make sure he didn't have any blood under his fingernails. He hoped he would never have to touch another body, but hoped he remembered to put on gloves if there was a next time.

There were invoices for gasoline and the electric bill for his cottage in his collection of paperwork. A mileage report for his work truck and a form for the hours he put on the outboard motor on his patrol boat. There were no spaces on any of the reports asking him how it made him feel to recover a body, get beat up, or lose a friend at sea.

Belker needed to go outside, and Hall walked with him out the dock and checked the lines on his patrol boat while Belker peed on his favorite bush. The moon had already set and the stars started at the horizon far out over Port Royal Sound and disappeared behind him in the limbs of the oaks and pines. The lights of Hilton Head glowed dully in the distance, and the surface of the water was so still and calm he wondered when he threw a sea shell into the water if the ripples would reach all the way to the ocean. He was sore and embarrassed from the fight he had gotten into. The fight he'd lost. The picture Detective Varnum emailed to him was the guy that had assaulted him. They were working on the same case and didn't even realize it until they met.

Long after sunrise he was still working on paperwork at his kitchen table when Varnum drove up in his unmarked police car. The detective suggested Hall's truck might attract less attention than his unmarked car, so Hall removed the magnetic USFWS emblems from the doors of his truck and put them under the driver's seat. Hall knew most people wouldn't notice the blue strobe lights concealed in the grille, and the tinted windows hid the equipment inside the cab.

"Expecting trouble?" Varnum asked when he saw the assault rifle locked in the gun rack.

"They issued it to me. I'd feel pretty stupid if I needed it out in the field and it was locked up in the safe in my house."

Varnum agreed and asked Hall to show to him where the key to the gun rack was hidden before they left. Without asking he rolled down his window and lit a cigarette as they drove under the Spanish moss and live oaks, leaving Pinckney Island and heading inland.

"Don't you think this guy will recognize me?" Hall asked the detective. He noticed when Varnum finished his cigarette he held it out the window and crumbled it between his fingers until all of the tobacco fell out and he put the filter in the pocket of his sport coat.

"I don't think he will. When you're in uniform that's all most people notice. I arrested someone who swore they'd kill me the next time they saw me and two days later I stood behind him in line at Wal Mart and he didn't remember me," Varnum said.

"What would you have done if he had?" Hall asked.

"I was wearing a sweat shirt and a pair of jeans with a .38 in my pocket. If I go past my mailbox I've got a gun close by," Varnum answered. "Just in case. How many refuge officers are there on Pinckney Island?"

"Just one, and he's pretty new," Hall said with a smile.

Varnum thought about that as they rode along together. A good cop never stopped learning. After he had finished the academy and rode with a coach for twelve weeks, he went to third shift and worked with a dozen other deputies who'd been on the job anywhere from two to twenty years. All of them had taught him something; sometimes it was what not to do, but he learned a lot from all of them. This kid was on his own.

"I've got a sample of the dirt from the construction site," Varnum said. He handed a plastic jar sealed with evidence tape to Hall.

"How did you do that?" Hall asked.

"A lot of dirt had spilled out of the dump truck onto the sidewalk and street. I stopped by and scraped up a little of it on my way over here."

Hall smiled in admiration and resolved to remember that there was usually more than one way to solve a problem.

"You never told me why you were looking for this guy," Hall said.

"An informant told me our suspect was coming into some big money, but she didn't know why. When I was checking him out I found a connection between him and a county inspector that was living beyond his means, and that led me to the construction site."

They passed Lemon Island and drove across the Broad River. Both men admired the view from the top of the bridge, the tallest vantage point in Beaufort County. They discussed their cases further, and Hall said he would check with the U.S. Attorney and see what federal charges could be brought against the developer and the county inspector. Varnum speculated that the driver of the black Trans Am would likely testify against the others in exchange for a lighter sentence.

"The barge and old warehouse are just down this road," Hall said.

They turned off the highway, and Hall showed Varnum where he'd hidden his truck the night before. Hall could feel his heart rate increase and wondered if he'd get another chance with the blonde suspect. In a fair fight he knew he could whip him. The two officers didn't talk as they drove down the dusty road.

"The barge is gone," Hall said when the building came into view. There were no vehicles parked anywhere they could see.

He parked far enough away from the old building so no one could look out of the window and see them, and they got out of the truck. Both men eased their doors closed. When they got to the end of the building there were no cars parked on the other side. They walked up to the door, which was standing open. Hall looked at the dock where he'd gotten into the fight and felt the muscles in his jaw flex.

"Sheriff's Office," Varnum called out. His voice echoed through the empty building. They each held a flashlight in their hands when they walked inside. They swept the building with the beams of light and Varnum nodded toward a small closet. He grabbed the edge of the door and nodded at Hall, who had his hand on his gun and his flashlight ready. Varnum flung the door open. The closet was empty.

"It looks like they moved out." Varnum was walking around the building, playing the beam of his flashlight over the floor.

"Is that blood?" Hall asked. Varnum looked at the spots on the floor and nodded. Then he saw a small plastic baggie on the floor.

"Drugs?" Hall asked. He'd had some basic narcotic identification classes, but had never seen the real thing other than some cocaine on a bathroom counter at a party while he was in college.

Detective Varnum pulled a pair of latex gloves out of the inside pocket of his sport coat and stretched them over his hands. With one hand he picked up the corner of a plastic baggie and with the other he fished a pair of glasses out and perched them on the tip of his nose.

"Crack, most likely. Hard to be certain without sending it to the lab. There would usually be more residue from the crystals if it was meth," Varnum answered. "If you ever suspect drugs are present, make sure you wear gloves. One of our deputies arrested a guy not long ago on a warrant for worthless checks. He had some plastic baggies and pills in his pocket, and the deputy confiscated them and packaged them to send to the lab. An hour later he was in the emergency room at Beaufort Memorial, smelling colors and seeing sounds. It was LSD. If he would have worn gloves when he searched his prisoner like he was supposed to, it never would have happened."

Hall was glad he always carried a pair of surgical gloves in a pocket on his bullet proof vest.

"We can't put it on anybody," Varnum said of the baggie, "So it's not worth sending to the lab. This place has been vacant for a long time. There's no telling who's been in here."

Hall went out to his truck and came back with his digital camera. He took pictures of the inside and outside of the warehouse and of the dock. At the end of the pier there were several clods of dirt and he collected a sample and put it in a plastic bottle similar to the one Varnum had given him.

Varnum noticed something on one of the dock pilings and showed Hall.

"It's mostly rust, but there is a little paint on this post."

Hall photographed the scrape of rust and paint and then scraped some of it off with his pocketknife and put it an evidence envelope.

"I wonder where they went," Hall said.

Chapter Thirty-Seven

Gale's scream triggered the "fight or flight" response in Arnold and he tried to back peddle out the door of the mobile home to escape but ended up tripping over the chain which was still attached to Gale's leg. He bounced down the wooden steps and into the front yard. Blondie pushed past Gale, and was on top of Arnold before he could get up. He slapped him across his face. Then he looked at Gale.

"You look pretty good for a dead woman."

Blondie got off Arnold and grabbed the chain that was attached to her ankle. He gave it a quick jerk and she tumbled down onto the floor. Her eyes were level with his while he stood on the ground.

"Maybe we can finish what I started when we first met."

Gale was trying to cry, to scream out in some way, but she felt like she'd had the wind knocked out of her and couldn't catch her breath. Blondie got close to her face and she smelled the liquor he'd been drinking. His left eye was swollen and he had a jagged cut on the end of his chin. She noticed his pupils were dilated and she wondered what he was on.

"You kids are getting pretty kinky, what with chains and all. Maybe we can get you and my friend to give us a show in a little while," Blondie said.

Gale looked at the stripper who was holding the flame from a cigarette lighter at the end of a clear glass tube and inhaling. Blondie leaned in closer and whispered in Gale's ear.

"You're already dead, but if you try to get away or tell her anything, I'll have to kill her too. You don't want to take guilt like that to your grave, do you?" Blondie asked Gale. Then he gripped the back of Gale's head, pulled her toward him, and forced his tongue inside her mouth. Gale gagged and spit when he finally released her.

After Blondie let go of Gale, he stepped over to Arnold, who hadn't moved since he'd been smacked around. He was breathing so hard Gale could hear him from several feet away. Blondie slapped Arnold again with his open palm just like Gale had watched him do at the warehouse. Arnold made no effort to defend himself, and Gale noticed his nose was bleeding again. Gale looked at the woman to see if she paid any attention to the violence. She was focused on her task and oblivious to what was going on around her.

"I can't believe you've been holding out on me like this, partner. What's mine is yours and what's yours is mine, right partner? I'll let you two have the master suite and my friend and I will have our little party here in the den. Then we can swap," Blondie said.

Arnold stood up and wiped the blood off of his face with the back of his hand. As he walked by, Blondie grabbed the keys for the truck out of his hand and pushed him down the narrow hallway of the trailer. Gale got up off the floor and followed him down the hall. The chain made a hollow sound as it dragged along the cheap tile floor behind her.

Inside the bedroom there was a bare, stained mattress on the floor and a small dresser. There were no lights in the room, and the only window was fogged with age. The bottom pane was broken out. Gale backed into a corner of the room and slid down the walls until she was sitting on the floor.

"You're already dead," she heard Blondie say over and over again in her mind. Ever since she'd been kidnapped, Gale had been able to convince herself that it would be over soon. She had believed Arnold was close to letting her go until this had happened. She wondered how Blondie had known where they were going or if he just got lucky.

Arnold was lying on his back on the filthy mattress, so still Gale thought he was asleep. Gale couldn't sleep. She wondered when Blondie was going to come back and what he was going to do to her when he did. From the noises spilling through the thin walls it sounded like the other girl was keeping him busy, and Gale hoped he stayed that way for a long time.

"How many other people in the world are getting ready for their death?" she wondered. Death row inmates, hospice patients. She couldn't think of any others and decided the number was very low. Death came as a surprise to most people. When she was on the hospital ship she had known people who were close to death. Some believed they were going to survive right up to their last breath, and others died in small increments, letting depression and fear rob them of their last moments of mortality. Gradually the fear left her and Gale began to feel at peace with her soul. Ever since she was a little girl in Sunday school she had known what was going to happen to her when she died and she had no reason to begin to doubt now. Knowing brought peace. Gale wanted to spend her last hours on earth remembering all of the things that made her happy, and she did.

Chapter Thirty-Eight

The next morning the telephone rang when Hall was in the shower and since the only phone in the house was on the wall in the kitchen, he had to stand in the kitchen and drip water everywhere while he talked. It was the dispatcher from the sheriff's department. They had received another anonymous tip about illegal netting. Hall wrote down the information and hung up the phone. The evidence he and Varnum had collected was on the kitchen table, and he put it all in his safe and spun the dial before he left his cottage.

"I've got to check out a tip, partner," he told Belker when he put him in the back yard. Maybe one day Belker could go out on patrol with him. That would help with the loneliness he sometimes felt when he was by himself for hours and hours on end. The pup barked once and then watched his master leave without further protests. Hall idled the patrol boat out of the narrow channel and looked around for the dolphin, but it wasn't there. He drove slowly around in a large circle when he reached deeper water, but still there was no sign of the dolphin. Maybe they got to sleep in every once in a while, he thought.

He turned toward the Broad River, and a boat along the far shoreline caught his eye. Someone was standing in the bow working a thin fly rod back and forth, and Hall could see the wispy line move in graceful loops back and forth until the fisherman leaned forward and with one last powerful thrust shot the line far out in front of the boat. Hall realized it was Silas, fishing by himself, and decided to watch for a few minutes.

The area Silas was fishing in was a mud flat that was completely dry for the last hour of the low tide. Hall avoided the area entirely for fear of becoming stranded and admired Silas for knowing how long he could stay there before the moon tugged the water away. While Hall watched, Silas stood motionless and leaned out over his feet, studying the water in front of him. He didn't move at all with the exception of his left hand which pulled in the line with short, quick jerks.

Suddenly he stood erect, held his fishing rod high in the air, and pulled the line tight. A few yards in front of the boat the calm water exploded, and Hall saw the sunlight reflect off the pink gills of a small fish. The fish jumped into the air once, twice, and on the third jump finally managed to free itself from the force that had seized it.

Across the water Hall heard Silas yell, a noise like a young boy might make when he rode his bicycle for the first time without training wheels. Silas saw Hall and waved. Hall waved back and gunned his boat up onto plane.

On the Broad River, just before he reached the highway bridge, he saw a small boat in the middle of the river. Hall changed his course to avoid rocking the smaller boat with his wake, but the lone occupant stood up and crossed his arms back and forth over his head.

Hall slowed and approached the boat. The man inside busied himself untangling a length of rope, and Hall noticed the motor cover was off the brand new outboard engine. Apparently he needed a tow. When the man looked up toward Hall again he dropped the rope he had been working with and sat down suddenly. As Hall got closer to the boat he saw the man fidgeting with something on the deck of the boat.

"Motor trouble?" Hall asked. He had drifted within a few feet of the stranded boater and was getting a line ready to throw to him.

"Yeah. It's brand new, too."

Hall nodded with sympathy and threw the man one of his lines from the patrol boat. Jimmy had taught him not to trust the condition of other people's equipment. The man showed some knowledge by securing the line to the bow eye of his boat instead of one of the cleats that might have torn free under the stress of towing.

"Where to?" Hall asked.

"Broad River Landing."

Hall was thankful that he would have to tow the boat less than two miles to the boat ramp. Maybe the illegal netters would still be in the area by the time he finished. Hall looked back to check on the boat in tow and thought the man seemed very nervous. Embarrassed. Hall understood. No one liked to get stranded on the water.

When they arrived at the boat ramp someone was launching his power ski, and

Hall remembered the dead girl from two nights ago. He realized he would remember her every time he heard the distinctive sound of the motorized water toys.

Five minutes later Hall pulled up to the floating dock, and the boat he was towing followed right behind. After he tied his patrol boat to the dock the man untied the tow rope and handed the line back to Hall.

"Thanks," he said. Then he turned and walked towards the parking lot, glancing back once at Hall. Hall put the tow line back where it belonged, cast off from the dock, and headed back to his original mission.

A half mile later Hall realized something he'd seen didn't make any sense. There were two large coolers in the boat he had towed in. Coolers that could hold a lot of fish, but he hadn't seen a single fishing rod. He wheeled his boat around so sharply that the engine over-revved when the propeller came out of the water and his boat slammed hard against its own wake.

Hall drove back to the boat ramp as fast as his boat would travel. The wind made his eyes tear, and anger burned in his throat. The guy in the boat was the same poacher that had outrun him in Hazzard Creek and had slogged through the mud to get away the day of the accident on the bridge. Hall was sure of it. The boat was different, but now he understood why the man was so nervous: he was afraid Hall would recognize him.

Hall ignored the no-wake buoy near the dock and headed toward the dock at full speed, slamming the engine into full throttle reverse at the last moment. The boat shuddered and strained but came to rest against the dock with a gentle thump. Hall jumped out of the boat and grabbed the bow line, tying it to the dock with a sloppy knot which would have earned a sharp rebuke from Jimmy Barnwell. When Hall saw the man he was facing away from him. The two coolers were on the ground next to his truck, and when Hall approached the man he grunted as he picked one up and set it on the tailgate. When he reached for the second cooler Hall slapped a handcuff on his wrist and jerked the man around so he was facing him.

"I don't want you to run away again," Hall said.

In the boat Hall found the illegal gill nets the man had used to catch thirty-two spottail bass and eighteen trout. Twenty of the fish were too small to possess, and that meant twenty separate charges in addition to charges of fishing with illegal gear, keeping more than the daily limit of trout and spottails, and fishing without a license. Hall seized the boat, the boat trailer, and the pick-up truck they were attached to. The statute dictated that upon conviction for these offenses the boat and truck would be sold at auction. Hall called for two wreckers to tow them both to the county impound lot.

A deputy arrived and transported the suspect to the Beaufort County jail for Hall. The charges against the suspect were state, not federal, but Hall hoped they were serious enough that no judge in the county would dismiss all of them. He was just a rookie but he had already experienced what could happen in court, regardless of guilt or innocence. When he thought about dismissed charges the image of the dead girl floating in the water came to him, but he quickly blinked it away.

The nets would be locked away until the trial as evidence, but the fish had to be photographed and disposed of. Hall chose to lay the illegal fish on the wooden dock to photograph. He lined up all fifty fish side by side and took pictures from several different angles. Other fishermen were launching and retrieving their boats and several stopped to ask him what was going on. Without exception, each one registered disgust with the acts of the poacher.

When he was finished collecting the evidence, he put the fish back into the coolers. The fish would spoil in the heat before he could take them anywhere, and he knew he would have to cut each one into pieces and dump all of them into the sound. Just as he loaded one of the heavy coolers into his boat someone on the dock behind him asked him a question.

"Whatcha gonna do with the fish?"

"I wanted to take them to the children's home at the Penn Center, but if they don't get on ice pretty quick they'll spoil."

Hall answered the question with his back to the man and when he turned around he recognized the man who had spoken to him.

"You picked up that boat I confiscated. Mr. Gallers, right?" Hall asked. He was ready for another confrontation.

"Yup. But as I recollect, you found my stolen boat," the old man said.

Hall had too much work waiting for him to waste time arguing, so he began to load the other cooler onto his boat.

"I hate to see all those fish go to waste," the old man said.

If the man was waiting for Hall to offer him some fish for the table he was wasting his time. He was convinced that the man was in cahoots with the poacher and would rather feed the fish to the sharks in the sound.

"If you'll wait a few minutes I'll git some ice," the old man said.

Hall wiped the river of sweat from his forehead and put his hands on his hips.

"Those kids would appreciate that," Hall said, "And so would I."

Without saying anything further the man walked over to his rickety old truck and came back with a half dozen bags of ice. In silence they each took the bags of ice, slammed them on the dock to break them up and poured the ice on top of the fish. When they were finished Hall collected the empty bags and put them in a trash can.

"Thanks," Hall said and stuck out his hand.

The man accepted the peace offering and took a foil pouch of chewing tobacco out of the pocket of his overalls. As he put a huge wad in his mouth, Hall thought it looked like he had a ping pong ball in his cheek.

"Well, I 'spect I'd better go see 'bout getting' my daughters' husband out of jail." It took Hall a moment to realize who he was talking about.

"I told him he couldn't use my boat no more, but he didn't care. Went an' bought a new motor for his ole boat. Said he could pay for it in a month selling the fish."

He spat in the water and Hall did his best to look humble and appreciative.

"Boy don't know nuthin' 'bout boat motors anyhow, otherwise he'd found that cut gas line a long time before you came along."

Hall thanked him again for the ice and for his help. The old man nodded and spat again.

"That was just too many fish. If he kept it up, there wouldn't be none left for nobody."

The heavy coolers took a few knots off of his top speed, but Hall made it to the Penn Center in just over forty minutes. He planned to give them the fish and go home as quickly as he could. He had worked through the weekend and the paperwork could wait until tomorrow. Maybe he could sleep in tomorrow, a thought that brought a smile to his face. When he went to Beaufort tomorrow to file a claim against the confiscated property he could eat at the diner next to the marina that Jimmy liked so much. Not a bad day so far, he thought, and it wasn't even noon yet.

Chapter Thirty-Nine

Mark Lancaster said he was pleased to come to the sheriff's headquarters to help with an investigation, but his body language said he was anything but happy to be there. Dark circles of sweat on his linen shirt were spreading from his underarms, and he kept biting his upper lip. Varnum thanked him for coming and sat across from him in an interview room that reeked of stale cigarette smoke even though tobacco use in county owned buildings had been banned years ago. Just as Varnum opened a thick folder, his cell phone rang. He excused himself and stepped out of the room, carrying the file.

On the other side of the two-way mirror Varnum watched his suspect fidget and sweat even more. Several times he pulled his cell phone out of his pocket but he never punched in any numbers. Varnum turned on the video recorder that was mounted behind the glass and confirmed that both video and audio in the room were being captured. When that was finished he went outside the building and smoked a cigarette.

When he came back inside he checked with a fellow detective and went back into the interview room. The real estate developer was startled by his entry and immediately stood up and started talking.

"I really don't have time for this, Detective. Am I a suspect or something? Should I call my lawyer?"

Varnum looked genuinely hurt and confused by this.

"A lawyer? Why would you think you need a lawyer, Mr. Lancaster? Why would you think you would be some kind of suspect?"

He walked over to Mark Lancaster. When he was in Lancaster's personal space, he sat on the edge of the table and tossed the heavy file on the table where it landed with a loud thunk.

"I just have a few questions about…"

The door to the interview room opened and Varnum stopped in mid-sentence. When he saw who was there he jumped off the table so quickly the file folder and its contents spilled on the floor.

"What the hell are you doing?" Varnum thundered. The detective Varnum had spoken to earlier was standing in the doorway and started to apologize. The county inspector who was with him saw Mark Lancaster sitting at the table in the interview room and looked liked he had just pissed in his pants.

"Get him out of here!" Varnum roared as he forcibly pushed them out of the room and slammed the door behind them. Then he picked up the scattered papers and left the room. On the other side of the door Mark Lancaster could hear him berating the other detective until their voices faded away. On the floor on the other side of the table Mark Lancaster saw a single sheet of paper that had fallen out of the detective's folder. From his hiding place behind the mirror Varnum watched his suspect glance at the door and then move out of his chair and pick up the piece of paper.

For a moment Varnum thought Mark Lancaster's eyes were going to pop out of his head. Then he heard his suspect moan through the speaker next to him. He must have read the handwritten notes Varnum had scribbled in the margin of the copy of the building permit: Twenty years for each charge, no parole and seizure of all personal and business assets under U.S. Federal Statute 53R.47-b. Varnum had made that up himself and scribbled it on the paper at the last minute. He thought it was a nice touch.

Before he went back in the interview to begin the long process of confession and soul cleansing, Varnum called the young game warden to see if he wanted to watch the interview. He left a message telling Hall he had some good news for him.

Chapter Forty

E ven though she had been out of her normal routine for over a week, Gale woke at five a.m. just as she had for as long as she could remember. Arnold was snoring heavily and a radio blared in another part of the trailer. Gale lay still and wondered how much longer she had. Her thoughts kept her busy for an hour until the sound of running water caught her attention. She put her ear against the thin wall and realized that Blondie was going to the bathroom. It sounded like he was having trouble hitting the commode, and she wondered if he was still stoned.

She waited to hear the toilet flush, but instead the door to the bedroom opened with a rush.

Blondie was standing in the doorway wearing only a pair of dirty blue jeans. He was barefoot and shirtless. For the first time she realized that even though he was a big man, his chest had no definition and his arms were flabby. He looked like the junkie he was.

Blondie stared at her and she stared right back. She was not going to spend the last precious minutes of life in fear. His eyes were bloodshot and wild and didn't waver from her. He stared at her for more than a minute, then glanced at Arnold who was still snoring heavily on the bed.

"Don't think I've forgotten about the last time we met," he said.

He took a step toward her and rubbed his crotch in a way that made her want to vomit. Another step and he began to unbutton his jeans. Gale put her hand to her mouth to stem the flow of bile she felt convulsing in her throat, but she swallowed, stood up and balled her fists. She was ready for the end and was going to face it on her own terms. He stepped closer to her and she swung at him with both arms as hard as she could. Her hands stung from blow after blow and she heard a terrible, growling scream coming from her own mouth.

His laughter hurt her more than the back of his hand that knocked her against the wall. He hit her again in her stomach and she felt like she was suffocating when she couldn't catch her breath. She slumped to the floor and he grabbed the chain in his hand and started to pull her toward him. Tears streamed down her face and she tried to scream but couldn't make a sound.

The force of the next punch knocked her on her back and her head bounced off the hard floor. Her face burned where the blood began to trickle from the corner of her mouth. He hit her in the face with his fist again and laughed as he straddled her, forced his knee between her legs, and pinned her to the floor. She closed her eyes and a sudden crushing weight knocked all the air out of her lungs again. She opened her eyes and saw Arnold on top of Blondie, hitting him with both fists so quickly his arms were a blur. She tried to squirm out from underneath them, but the weight was too great and she couldn't move. Again and again Arnold hit him, and the sound of the blows was sickening even though she knew they meant she had been spared, at least for the moment.

The two men rolled off her, and she managed to scramble onto the nasty mattress as they continued to battle on the dirty, cramped floor. Throughout it all Arnold stayed on top of Blondie, but the smaller man refused to be beaten. Blondie screamed when Arnold's knee drove into his groin with enough force to move him several inches across the floor. Blondie's skinny arms flailed again and again against Arnold's large body, but they had no effect. Then Gale saw the knife.

It was shiny and silver for only an instant, then it was crimson with blood. Blondie thrust and slashed wildly, and blood splattered onto the walls and the ceiling. Blood splashed onto her face, but she couldn't escape. Both men blocked the tiny door out of the bedroom.

Arnold continued to fight. He knocked the knife from Blondie's hand, but the damage had been done. He was so bloody from punctures to his chest and cuts on his shoulders that his blows slipped off Blondie's face with less effect each time he struck. Bright red, aerated blood bubbled from his nose and mouth, and Gale knew his lung had been pierced. He wouldn't last much longer.

Blondie pulled himself out from underneath the body when Arnold died. Gale could not control herself any longer and vomited when Blondie picked up his knife and plunged it into Arnold's dead body over and over again. When he was done he looked silently at Gale. His breathing was heavy and erratic and his eyes were wide with rage. He stumbled out of the bedroom. Gale looked up and saw the blonde girl in the doorway staring at Arnold, then at Gale.

It seemed for a moment that she was alright with what happened. She kept nodding her head up and down as if she was agreeing with a question no one had asked.

"Hey," the girl said to Arnold. "Are you OK?"

"He's dead," Gale said. "Run!"

Her head bobbed up and down again but she didn't move."Is he OK?" she asked.

Then her head changed direction and began to shake from side to side. Her eyes seemed to open wider and her breathing changed to choking gasps. Gale heard her run through the trailer and then a door slammed.

Gale moved to the edge of the bed to look at Arnold lying on the floor. She closed her eyes and rocked back and forth on her knees with her hands clasped together so tightly that her fingers began to throb with pain and she felt every beat of her heart in the wounds on her face.

When she finally opened her eyes and wiped away the tears, she realized she was covered with blood. Hers, Arnold's, Blondie's. She felt the inside of her mouth with her tongue. A few of her teeth were loose. Her left eye was almost swollen shut and her vision was blurred. She thought she might have a concussion. She had survived yet again, but Arnold had not.

She looked at his body and did not understand. He had held her prisoner for almost two weeks. Twice he had saved her from death, and she never knew why. She didn't even know his last name. He had never defended himself against Blondie, but he fought to the death to protect her. Who was he?

Chapter Forty-One

H all's plan to get back home as soon as he could was a good one, but it didn't quite work out that way for him. Everyone at the Penn Center, including the kitchen staff, was at the worship service when he arrived. The heat was oppressive, the humid, early-summer air confirming the promise of afternoon thunderstorms. He waited in the shade of a century-old live oak for someone to arrive, and after a while an old man came out of the sanctuary carrying the offering baskets. When he saw Hall he motioned for him to follow him into the kitchen.

It was at least ten degrees hotter in the kitchen. Three large, institutional-grade ovens were hard at work, and whatever was inside them smelled delicious. When he finished checking on lunch the old man gave Hall a tall glass of iced tea and they went around to the back of the building and began to clean the fish.

They worked together without conversation and several more men joined them at the long wooden table. Hall guessed that most of them were in their eighties and noticed their large, strong hands moving without effort with the slippery fish. These were hands that had tonged oysters and thrown nets for shrimp and fish for decades. How they felt about the changes they had lived through, Hall could only imagine. The islands they had been born on were now gated and fenced luxury communities. Every day there were fewer farms, and shrimp houses were replaced by fancy marinas overnight. Luxury cruisers outnumbered hand made skiffs more than one hundred to one, and most of their children, grandchildren, and great-grandchildren lived in cities far away. Hall felt like an intruder, not because he was the only white person there, but because he was from another world.

Soon they were finished, and Hall realized that while he looked like a war casualty, not one of the men had a single bloodstain on their white dress shirts. He was too hungry to pass up an invitation to stay for lunch and knew it would have been impolite to refuse the homemade desserts. He left with a piece of pound cake wrapped in waxed paper and promised to come by for lunch again soon. Once he was alone on his boat he took off his gun belt and adjusted it one space larger. He was embarrassed but felt much better and like he wouldn't need to eat again for several days. The tide had dropped during his stay, and despite his best efforts, he ran aground within sight of the sound. He prodded the bottom with a boat hook and realized the bottom was so soft and gooey he would sink past his knees if he tried to push the boat off the sandbar.

After checking the tide chart he thought he should float free in a little over an hour or so. He positioned himself so that he was in the shade from the T-top and looked at the tall cumulus clouds that were building inland, to the east. One massive group of clouds was beginning to flatten out on top, and he wondered if the thunderstorm would form on top of him or out over the ocean.

He sat and watched the muddy sandbar begin to rise from the water as the tide dropped even further. At the water's edge several immature roughtail stingrays fed with their domed backs and slotted eyes protruding from the water. They looked like aliens as they made gentle slurping noises and shuttled along the muddy waterline feeding on small minnows and shrimp.

He opened his eyes when a dolphin blew close to his boat. A much better navigator, the dolphin swam only a few feet away from Hall where the water was deep enough for it and deep enough for the patrol boat to float if he had only taken that route. Hall stood and shaded his eyes against the sun and tried to see if he recognized the dolphin. "His" dolphin had the scar on its neck from the fishing net and there was another with a propeller scar on its dorsal fin he'd seen at several locations in Port Royal Sound. His schooling told him the sound and the surrounding waters could support hundreds of the mammals, but he also knew dolphins could recognize the sounds of individual boats. They knew the difference between a shrimp boat that would soon be culling its catch and a passenger ferry that traveled the very same route. Hall wondered if the dolphins recognized his boat when he sped past them. They probably referred to it as the boat that got stuck a lot, he thought.

Soon the dolphin moved on and the stingrays quit feeding at the waters edge. The spartina grass dancing in the shimmering heat was not enough to hold his attention and he fell asleep with his chin on his chest.

When Blondie came back into the bedroom he had on a clean pair of khaki pants and a golf shirt that once had been white but was now a dingy gray with yellowed bleach stains. His face was puffy and swollen and his hands were stained pink where he had not been able to wash away the blood. When he walked toward the bed he limped and Gale prayed Arnold had crushed his testicles. Without saying anything he grabbed her chain and turned back around, pulling her out of the bedroom. She had to step over Arnold's body on the way out of the room, trying to keep up with Blondie so he didn't pull her off her feet with the chain.

The girl, whoever she was, was gone. There were liquor bottles on the floor and some empty plastic baggies on the kitchen table. His bloody blue jeans were piled on the floor next to a red plastic gasoline can. Blondie grabbed it when he walked by and headed for the front door. She watched him pour gasoline on the carpet, throw down a lighted match, and felt the heat when the fumes ignited with a whoosh. He closed the flimsy front door and made her climb through the driver's door of the same truck Arnold had driven to the trailer yesterday.

"Get down," he said. He was hard to understand with his mouth and cheeks swollen, but she knew what he wanted her to do. She sat down on the passenger floorboard and pulled her knees close to her chest. After lighting a cigarette, Blondie put a sandwich bag with ice in it on his lap and put the truck into gear with a lurch.

By watching shadows and catching a glimpse of the sun, Gale reasoned they were going back to the barge. The boat must be the only link to him, she guessed. He needed to get rid of the contaminated soil and sell the boat before he could disappear. The ocean would hide her body as well. A few minutes after they turned onto the paved road she heard a fire truck pass with its siren screaming. Burning the mobile home hid the evidence of the murder, at least for a while, and had the added bonus of attracting all the attention. No one would notice her boarding the barge, so she wouldn't be missed when Blondie returned without her.

She thought her buttocks were numb from the cramped ride, but when the truck bounced over a pothole as they pulled into the parking lot of the marina, a sharp pain shot through her hips and up her back. Blondie sat in the truck drawing heavily on the cigarette with every other breath. He threw it out when it burned down to the filter and lit another one right away. She stole several glances at him, trying to guess what he was going to do next and wondering why he hadn't left her chained to the bed when he set the place on fire. Gale knew it really didn't matter, but she did take a small measure of solace in knowing her final resting place would be the sea, a place she loved more than any other. Sitting in the sweltering heat of the rusty old truck she could smell the marsh, the scent of fish and crabs that had been etched into the wooden docks, and the smell of approaching rain. A gull protested loudly against some unseen tormentor. The same yesterday, today, and tomorrow even if she wouldn't be here to appreciate it.

Halfway through his third cigarette another fire truck roared past and Blondie opened his door. He pulled on the chain and indicated for her to follow him. Once she was out of the truck, she looked around the small gravel parking lot. There were several pick-up trucks with empty boat trailers parked near the oyster-shell boat ramp, but no one was here. The bait shop was closed, and Gale realized it was Sunday. Two decades ago it would have been illegal for the bait shop to be open on a Sunday, but the "Blue Laws' had been legislated into extinction when she was a little girl. For most people Sunday was no longer God's day. It was just another day to sleep late, go fishing, or watch a ball game.

Gale had been born on a Sunday. She knew that because her mother had saved the Savannah Daily News from the day she had been born. Because of the hurricane that had raged on her birthday, the Beaufort Gazette didn't have an edition on that Sunday and wasn't published again until she was a week old when the water had receded and the electricity had been restored. The first post-hurricane edition announced the arrival of Beaufort's newest citizen, Gale Ruth Pickens. She could not know the same newspaper had printed her obituary just a few days ago.

The handcuff dug into Gale's raw ankle, and she walked awkwardly across the dock as Blondie pulled on the chain. He was limping and grunting in pain when he climbed over the boat railing. He took her into the pilot house and ran a bolt though the chain that he looped around an exposed pipe. Blondie tightened the bolt with the same greasy crescent wrench that he'd hit her with when they'd first met. He disappeared below decks, and she heard him hammering on something and then felt the old diesel struggling to turn over. Finally the old motor coughed and wheezed and belched nasty black fumes into the air.

A few minutes later Blondie climbed out and loosed the barge from the dock. Gale noticed he left the lines lying on the dock when he untied the boat. When the boat lurched away from the dock Gale felt a solid bump and heard a loud crack when the planking gave way to the heavy mass of the boat. Blondie responded by increasing the throttle. Finally clear of the obstacle, the boat entered into the wide river channel and turned into the wind.

Chapter Forty-Two

A distant rumble nudged Hall back into consciousness. When he opened his eyes it took him a moment to orient himself. The bright summer sun was gone, and the wind on his face was cool and pleasant. When he looked behind him he saw where the wind was going.

Above him a massive cumulonimbus thundercloud sucked air into its base while forty thousand feet higher the dark, black cloud flattened out against the cooler air of the upper troposphere. Inside the storm cloud, warm and humid air rose to the top of the cloud until the moisture accumulated into raindrops and then froze into hailstones when they passed into yet colder, higher air. With violent speed the air mass within the cloud suddenly shifted directions and began to race back towards the earth, carrying the rain drops and ice crystals in the violent downdraft.

The first flash of lightning awed Hall with its beauty, and he saw the streak pulse as the raw energy passed back and forth between the cloud and the ground. He lowered the antennas on his boat and barely got his slicker on before the rain started. He saw it come across the water in sheets and felt it on his cheeks. Then hail began to fall and ricocheted off of the deck of the boat and stung his bare legs. The boat was still stuck on the sandbar, but there was enough water under the stern of the boat for him to start the engine. Lightning flashed again, much closer this time, and he had only counted to ten when thunder clapped in his ears.

Hall put the engine into reverse and used his body weight to rock the boat from side to side until it slid free from the mud. Once he was far enough away from the shoal he shifted into forward and tried to see into the wall of water that was falling from the sky.

The lightning concerned him the most. He knew a thunderstorm could produce winds that were strong enough to flip his boat over, but that was unlikely. The aluminum frame of his boat top towered above the water and marsh grass like a giant lightning rod, and for once he was grateful for the inflatable life jacket he was required to wear. He wanted to reach the river and head toward Beaufort. There were several homes along the water in that direction, and he would tie up to the first dock he came to and wait out the storm. Visibility decreased to the point where he could see less than ten feet in front of his boat. The hail became more intense and stung the back of his hands as he clung to the wheel. He couldn't see the edge of the marsh anymore and steered his boat by watching the depth finder, keeping his boat in the deeper water in the middle of the creek.

He knew he had reached the river when the waves began to pound against the front of his boat, and the wind tried to push him sideways. He continued out into the river for a few yards and then turned his boat to starboard until his compass pointed north/northeast. He traveled just fast enough to maintain a course against the wind and the waves and strained to see something other than whitecaps and bolts of lightning. When he turned slightly more to the north the rain seemed to lessen, and he was able to see fifty or so feet in front of the boat. He reached for the throttle to increase his speed, but when he pushed it forward the motor stopped.

With the noisy outboard quieted Hall heard the full fury of the storm for the first time. Lightning flashed, and the crash of thunder was instantaneous. Hall knew he was in trouble. He took the anchor from the locker and slipped it into the water. As the line slipped through his wet hands, a strong wave rocked the boat and he was almost thrown overboard. He dropped to his knees and played out the line. The anchor hit the bottom fairly quickly, but Hall let out all two hundred feet of rope before he cleated it off on the windward side of the bow.

He crawled back to the motor and tilted it out of the water to see what was wrong. When the propeller came out of the water he saw it was choked with weeds, and he was grateful it was such a minor problem. He began to pull the weeds and grass away from the propeller and cut his finger on one of the knife-sharp blades. Just as he got the last of the grass off of the propeller, a wave rolled into the back of the boat and drenched him.

The anchor wasn't holding and the boat was taking the waves against her stern, the lowest part of the boat. Gallons of heavy water rushed in and Hall knew the boat would swamp if he took many more waves like that one. Another wave came into the boat and Hall tilted the motor back into the water and turned the key. The battery was strong and the engine turned over willingly but would not start. Hall looked at his depth gauge and watched the water get deeper and deeper. He was being pushed out into Port Royal Sound toward the open Atlantic Ocean.

Gale saw the lightning flash and without thought began counting. The storm was getting closer, and she wondered in which direction it was headed. There was no wind flowing into the stagnant pilothouse of the barge, and Gale reasoned the storm was behind them and believed it would soon overtake the slow barge on its path to the sea. Gale knew Blondie was getting ready to do something when he began to look around in every direction. She knew it was time.

"Stand up," Blondie ordered.

She stood and stretched her arms and legs. Arnold's blood stained her warm up suit and her running shoes. She looked out the window and saw she had been right about the storm. It was going to catch them. A slight breeze came through the open door, and she smelled rain on the wind. The smell of rain always brought a smile to her face. She inhaled deeply through her nose and closed her eyes.

Blondie had a greasy crescent wrench in his hand and hit Gale on the back of her head as hard as he could. She fell against a window and her lip burst against the glass, smearing it with blood. She landed in an awkward jumble on the steel deck with blood pouring from her scalp. He drew back with the wrench to hit her again, but stopped. He remembered the blood from Arnold, all over the bedroom and all over him. He didn't bring a change of clothes on the boat.

After unfastening the chain from the pipe, Blondie dragged Gale's limp body from the wheelhouse and threw her down into the hopper area of the boat, on top of the last load of dirt. He took the blue plastic tarp and pulled it over her body just as the rain and hail began to fall.

Panic began to rise in Hall's throat. The waves were getting stronger and pounded the small craft so hard Hall kept getting knocked to his knees. He tightened the straps on his life preserver and reached for the marine radio.

"Any station, any station, any station. This is Foxtrot-Whiskey-Sierra 3-4-9 requesting assistance."

Hall un-keyed the microphone and waited for a response. The Coast Guard, Beaufort County Sheriff's Office, and dozens of commercial and private craft monitored the emergency channel day and night, but no one responded. Hall tried his broadcast several more times, forgetting that he had folded down his antenna in preparation for the storm. As a result his radio signal was only traveling a few yards from his boat.

When Hall finally realized no one heard his calls for help he began to calm down. He assessed his situation, starting with the worst case scenario: capsizing or swamping. The water temperature was in the mid-seventies, so hypothermia would be hours away. The wind was pushing him east, into the ocean, but the tide was stemming his progress somewhat. There was enough foam floatation under the bow and console of the boat to keep it from sinking even if it was upside-down. He crawled to the bow locker and took a dock line out of it. If the boat did go over, he wanted to stay with it. A boat was a lot easier to find than a single small human being, bobbing in the waves. He tied the line to the seat post and coiled the rest of it on the deck next to him, ready to grab if he needed to.

After ten minutes Hall began to wonder how big the storm was. He was still being stung by wind and hail, and the waves were still steep and large. Then he saw the edge of the storm, a faint line of light underneath the black clouds. But the edge of the storm never moved closer, and he realized he was caught in the storm and was moving with it out to sea. He was at its mercy until it ran out of energy.

Chapter Forty-Three

Blondie was going to beat the storm. The engine on the old barge was running smoothly, and he was going to make it out of Port Royal Sound and into the Atlantic before the wind picked up to any degree. Since the storm was coming from inland, he planned to turn south and let the land mass of Hilton Head Island shelter him from the brunt of the storm. This was his last load and he would wait an hour or so, until twilight, and dump his cargo just off the beach. The dirt and chemicals would foul the beach, and he wondered what early rising beachcomber would find the body.

With the exception of his horribly swollen testicles and bruised face, everything was going well. He had almost fifty grand in cash, and his Trans Am was stashed at a hotel in Savannah. He didn't have a partner to split the proceeds with any longer, and as soon as the load was gone he would take the barge to a broker in Beaufort and wait for a check to arrive in his post office box. There was nothing at the trailer that led back to him except for the stripper who ran away, but she had no idea who he really was. Wherever he ended up he would use another name, become someone else, hang out at topless clubs and wait for opportunity to come knocking. It always did. There were always people out there who needed someone else to do their dirty work for them.

Blondie had made the trip out of the sound several times with Arnold, and even though he had never piloted the boat he paid attention just in case he ever got pissed off enough to actually throw Arnold overboard. That was paying off now. He saw the edge of the island to his right and waited until he was far enough past the beach to begin his turn. Arnold always followed the line of buoys out to sea, but there was no need for him to do that now. He wanted to drop the load in close to shore, drop off the boat, and get out of town.

As the boat began to swing around, Blondie noticed the motion of the waves for the first time. He attributed it to the wind from the storm, but he was wrong. By not following the marked channel out into the ocean he was cutting across Joiner Banks. Five hours from now, when the tide was full, there would be ten feet of water over the shoals. Since the barge only needed six feet of water to float, he would have slipped right over the shallow bottom without any problem at all. But now there was only two feet of water above the sandbar and the bottom of the barge plowed into the sand and mud.

With the wind, the current, and waves Blondie didn't immediately realize he was in trouble. Since the engine was still engaged, the energy from the prop pushed the stern of the barge to the left and it wasn't until Blondie saw the beach houses of Port Royal Plantation directly ahead that he realized something was wrong.

Unlike an outboard or stern-drive boat, on which the propeller actually moved left and right to steer a boat, the barge had a fixed propeller directly in front of a large rudder. Steerage was accomplished by deflecting the flow of the water against the blade of the rudder. Since the barge was aground there was no flow of water past the rudder and turning the wheel had no effect at all. When he realized that the barge wasn't responding to the wheel, Blondie redlined the engine and pushed himself further on the sandbar. By the time he thought to reverse the engine he was already stuck fast.

He put the engine in neutral, stepped out of the pilothouse and realized what he had done. His curse was drowned out by a tremendous peal of thunder. The lightning was so close when Blondie finally caught his breath from the scare he could smell the ozone in the air.

He was more angry than scared. There wasn't enough water to float his barge, much less sink it. He was only two-hundred yards from shore, and by the looks of things he could have walked to the beach and not gotten his shoulders wet. But he couldn't abandon ship because he didn't want anyone to put the contaminated soil, the dead bitch, and the barge all together. Too many people had seen him on the boat when they fueled it up or when they docked in Beaufort for repairs. The cops might look for him for a little while for abandoning a boat and dumping some contaminated dirt, but they would look a lot harder and longer for a murder suspect.

He had no idea if the tide was rising or falling or what the wind from the impending storm might do. He only knew he had to move the boat soon, before some nosey do-gooder on the beach reported a boat stranded on the shoals. Wouldn't those crew-cut young Coasties get a big kick out of finding him with a dead body when they boarded the barge to help him out? He reached for the throttle to try and reverse off of the sandbar one more time, but his hand brushed the hydraulic lever for the hopper and he knew how to make his boat float once again.

Every time they had dumped a load of contaminated soil Blondie had noticed the barge shuddered and shook as the dirt fell out of the bottom of the hopper. One day when he had loaded soil onto the barge he noticed how much lower the boat rode in the water when it was full of dirt. It was a significant difference. All he had to do was release the load now, and he could float back into the sound. The way the storm looked no one would be out on the beach to find the body until morning anyway.

Blondie nudged the boat into reverse, but kept the throttle at idle speed. When he floated free he wanted just enough speed to clear the sandbar. He grabbed the hopper control and moved it to "release", but the barge didn't shudder or shake or float off of the sandbar. The only thing he noticed was the hissing sound coming from below decks: The hydraulic fitting had failed again. Blondie unleashed a torrent of curses and picked up the bloody wrench from the deck. He opened the hatch to the engine room and climbed down into the dingy, dark compartment.

Hall continued to move with the storm at about fifteen knots, headed due east. In front of him he could see nothing but black sky. Behind him he saw an occasional glimpse of light gray. He didn't think he was out of the sound and into the ocean yet, but knew he had to be close. A hailstone had fractured the screen of his depth finder, so now that reference was gone as well. While he drifted, the boat stayed mostly bow-to the wind thanks to the drag from the dangling anchor, and he tried several more times to start the motor without success. Hall sat on the deck behind the console and was shielded from the worst of the rain and hail while he looked and prayed for the break in the storm he knew would eventually come.

When his boat slammed into the stranded barge he flew sideways and smashed his nose against the engine cowling. His blood tasted coppery on his tongue. When his eyes focused he turned to see what he'd struck and saw a black and rusty metal wall towering above his boat. Although he wasn't sure what happened he scrambled to his feet and grabbed the line from beside him on the deck. It appeared he had blown into an anchored boat, and he wanted to tie his patrol boat to it before the wind pushed him away. The rails on the barge were too high for him to reach, and there was nothing else on the side of the boat to secure his line to. The wind was pushing him along the side of the anchored boat, slamming it hard enough that Hall heard the fiberglass hull of his boat crack and pop every time they came together. In a few seconds he would scrape past the end of the boat and would be adrift again. He had to do something right now.

Chapter Forty-Four

B londie heard a thump against the barge, but the thick steel hull and several tons of dirt muffled the sound, and he was too occupied with the stubborn fitting to worry about what the noise was. Finally, after scraping his knuckles and rounding off one of the bolts that secured the hydraulic hose, he thought he had fixed it.

He crawled out of the hatch and was surprised by how cold the rain was and how much the small hailstones hurt. He could no longer see the shore and could barely see the bow of the boat, only forty-odd feet from the pilothouse. This time he heard and felt the noise at the same time. He looked forward, and halfway to the front of the boat someone in a bright yellow rain coat was pulling himself onto the barge. The person was tying a rope to the railing and when a gust of wind blew his raincoat open, Blondie saw a gun and a badge.

The barge wasn't pitching and rolling like his patrol boat had been, but it still took Hall a moment to adjust to the rocking of the larger vessel. He scanned the deck and all he saw was a large blue plastic tarp and the pilot house aft. Several parts of the tarp were loose and the wind was threatening to rip the entire covering loose. Hall started to walk across the tarp and lost his footing on the slick and uneven surface. He began to fall and braced himself for a hard landing. His knees hit first, but instead of a hard jolt he was relieved to find a cushioned landing. A strong chemical odor caught in his nose.

Hall stood up, only to fall again, and decided to crawl the rest of the way to the pilothouse. He got ready to climb up to the raised portion of the boat and the tarp in front of him tore loose in the wind and began to attack him. The metal grommet in the tarp stung his face and hands, and he struggled to crawl past it. The weight of his body finally subdued the errant tarp and he crawled over the edge of it into the muddy dirt it had been covering.

With perfect clarity Hall knew this was the barge he had been searching for. They must have anchored the boat here and abandoned it, even if he didn't know where "here" was. As soon as the storm cleared he would call for help and find out who owned the boat. He had them now! His feelings of triumph vanished when the wind picked up the tarp again, and he saw a bloody human head lying in the dirt.

It was Gale! How could it be? He tried to find her pulse at the carotid artery in her neck but felt nothing. She was cold and gray, and he was afraid she was dead. There was a gash on the back of her head where her scalp was torn, and he noticed with relief that it was bleeding, but in slow, irregular pulses. He rolled her on her side and air rushed out of her lungs. He thought she was close to bleeding to death, by the amount of blood on her shirt and pants. With nothing else available, Hall took his life jacket off and quickly used his pocketknife to cut off one of the sleeves of his raincoat. He cut it into strips and tied it around her head as tightly as he could.

Lightning flashed again, and he knew whoever did this to Gale had to still be on board. He looked around, and decided to get Gale to a safer location before investigating further. Her body was completely limp, and he struggled to lift her out of the hopper and up onto the deck. He was still standing in the mud when he realized he was sinking.

Blondie was in the pilothouse, peeking over the wheel and out the window. When he saw the cop start to walk across the tarp, he laughed and pulled the release lever again. The crabs would get to eat twice as much tonight, he thought, but the barge didn't shudder and drop the dirt as he expected. He felt the boat bump up and down on the sandbar and realized it was keeping the hopper doors from swinging open. He increased the throttle and peered out the window again.

Hall decided he was imagining things, that his feet must have slipped deeper into the mud. He hoisted himself up onto the deck next to Gale and drew his gun, heavy and awkward in his hand. Within a few seconds his forearm began to ache and he realized he was squeezing the pistol too hard. He forced himself to relax his gun hand. The rain continued to fall at a sharp angle and felt like sand as it stung his arms and face. He felt chilled without his raincoat, but he shivered from the adrenaline, not the cold.

Step by step he worked his way closer to the pilothouse. The barrel of the pistol was his third eye, leading him as he scanned with it and searched for suspects. The small pilothouse was the only place on the boat someone could be unless they were down in the engine room. Just as he reached for the door handle it was sucked away and someone jumped out in front of him. Hall stumbled backward in surprise.

"Don't shoot!" Blondie yelled.

He startled Hall so badly that he would have shot him if his finger had been on the trigger. He caught himself hyperventilating.

"Hands up!" Hall yelled back into the wind.

It was a stupid thing to say. The man's hands were already stretched high above his head. He was walking toward him and almost seemed to be crying. Hall understood bits and pieces of what he said as the wind snatched away the rest

"Highjacked.....beaten..........killed that poor girl."

The man was walking toward him and still had his hands in the air. He was sobbing now. The blonde-headed man did look like he'd been in a fight. One of his eyes had a bluish-black crescent under it and his face was scratched and swollen. He was limping and had blood on his clothing.

"Help me," the man said. Hall was close enough to understand him now and recognized the man he'd fought with a few days ago.

Hall was not ready for the sudden move, and he froze. Blondie grabbed the gun with both of his hands and drove his forehead into the bridge of Hall's already injured nose. Hall felt the cartilage in his nose crack and gripped his gun as hard as he could with both of his hands.

The fight started hard from the beginning. There was no foreplay of pushing and shoving, no threats or posturing. They both knew only one of them would live to see the end of the storm. On the defensive from the beginning, all Hall could do was concentrate on holding onto his gun. A sudden wave made the barge lurch sideways and they were both thrown hard against the metal railing. Blondie slammed his head into Hall's face again and tried to do it a third time but Hall moved to the side just in time. Hall tasted more blood but felt no pain. He put his head down and pushed against Blondie's chest like a boxer and watched the barrel of the gun swing wildly back and forth as they both struggled for control. The front sight played across Hall's leg, across the deck and over Blondie's foot. When the front sight was lined up with the pair of sneakers again, Hall pulled the trigger three times as fast as he could.

Blondie screamed with pain but didn't let go. One of the bullets entered his right shin just below his knee and traveled down his leg, shattering the bone as it went. Blondie didn't loosen his grip on the gun, but the bone structure to support his weight was no longer there. He began to fall and pulled Hall down with him. Together they tumbled over the railing and into the mud and sand in the hopper. When Hall fell he saw Gale lying in the rain on the deck and knew he was fighting for her life as well.

Hall landed on top of Blondie. Four hands fought for the gun. Taking a chance, Hall let go with his left hand and began to punch Blondie as hard as he could in the face and throat and then in the ribs. When his hand hurt from punching he used his elbow like a hammer. He was hitting Blondie so hard that he felt the man's ribs crack as he pummeled away, and it seemed to be working. Blondie seemed to get weaker. Hall quit hitting him and wrapped his free hand around Blondie's throat and squeezed as hard as he could.

The effect was instantaneous. Blondie released one of his hands from the pistol and tried to peel Hall's fingers from his neck. Within another few seconds he quit fighting for the gun altogether and was trying with both hands to get loose from the death-grip on his neck. When the gun was free Hall put the barrel in Blondie's side and tried to pull the trigger, but nothing happened. He glanced down at the gun and saw the trigger guard caked with mud. He dropped the useless tool and used both hands to strangle Blondie. He heard one man roar with anger and another man gasp for his final breath. He didn't stop when he crushed his windpipe and he didn't stop when Blondie began to violently convulse and heave. He squeezed and squeezed as hard as he could for a long time after Blondie quit moving.

Hall stood over Blondie and felt a rage he had never felt before. He knew he had to get past his anger and the questions he had if he wanted to save Gale. There was much less light now as twilight approached. The worst of the storm had passed, and Hall stood up to look for Gale. She was still lying on the steel deck beside the pilot house, and he started to walk toward her across the uneven soil in the hopper. Just then the moon pushed the tide inland. Only a fraction of an inch, just enough to clear the barge from the sandbar and into deeper water. Hall felt the barge shudder and then the ground was sucked out from underneath him. Everything went black.

Chapter Forty-Five

As she struggled to breathe she realized she was going to die. A man in a uniform lay near her on the muddy sandbar, and she wondered if he was dead already. She had tried to save him. She knew it would be six more hours before the tide would rise again. Too late.

She had lived her life by the tides for as long as she could remember. The water flowed higher and swifter during the full and new moons, slower and softer during the quarters. The rhythm of her life. The moon illuminated both of them, lying together near the waters edge. Her gray, bare body shivered from hypothermia and she died as the moon rose over Pinckney Island.

The Palmetto Room in the governor's mansion was one of the smaller rooms in the enormous structure. It was considered part of the residence, and as such was not commonly used for official business. The mahogany-paneled walls, wildlife prints and brick fireplace gave the room the feel of a southern gentleman's study. Outside the temperature on the first day of summer topped the century mark. The governor, wearing khakis and a denim shirt, entered the room with one of his aides.

"My job is to help the people of South Carolina. Better education. Smarter laws. A higher standard of living. Everything I do to accomplish those ideals takes place in safe, air-conditioned buildings. Like most of our citizens, I take our clean air and pristine waters for granted. My family and I are able to enjoy the natural beauty of our state thanks to men and women who protect the environment from dangers we could never imagine. Gale Pickens is one of our protectors," he said.

Gale slipped her hand out of Hall's and stood next to the governor. Most of the bruising was gone from her face, but her left eye had a few broken blood vessels that refused to heal quickly. The marks on her ankle were only visible when she wasn't wearing socks and her thick hair covered the scar on the side of her head. The unseen scars were healing too.

The body of Linwood Thompkins was never found. Detective Varnum had been able to identify Blondie from fingerprints he left on the barge and in his car. Hall wanted the closure seeing the body for himself and for Gale, but was satisfied that the very environment he had been poisoning would be his final resting place. Harold Peterson and Mark Lancaster were both in the Beaufort County Detention Center, and Hall was under subpoena to testify in the upcoming trial.

Gale's brother Silas, Ted and Rebecca Barnwell, and Hall's boss Susan Charles were at the ceremony. Ted gave Hall an approving nod and smile when they looked at each other. As far as Hall was concerned, that was better than an award from any politician.

The governor rattled on for a few minutes about the history of the Order of the Palmetto, remembering previous recipients and their accomplishments.

"Gale has dedicated her life to preserving our coastal waters, making sure they are protected for future generations...."

On the southeastern side of Dawes Island, in the middle of Port Royal Sound, is a beach of beautiful white sand. It is ringed with oyster bars and spartina grass, and the live oaks and palmettos break the ocean breezes. Tonight there was a group of people on the normally deserted strip of sand.

Two small boats were beached nearby, a fishing skiff and a center console with Soundkeeper scripted on her bright yellow hull. Gale and Carl Varnum were seated on blankets around a huge picnic basket, and plates and cups were scattered around a dying driftwood campfire. Further up the island two men and a young Labrador retriever were walking slowly toward the moon that looked like it was rising out of the ocean. When they reached the water's edge, one of them spoke.

"I wanted to bring you here to show you this."

Silas opened the burlap oyster bag he was carrying. He reached inside and pulled out the skull of an animal. Hall recognized it as the skull of a bottle nosed dolphin.

"Take off your shirt," Silas said.

Hall pulled his T-shirt over his heard. The scabs on his shoulder were all gone and the dozen small pink dots would be scars soon. Silas opened the jaw of the skull he was holding and put Hall's shoulder inside of it. The teeth matched up perfectly with the marks on his arm.

Hall took the skull from Silas and held it against his arm. Each tooth matched up with another set of marks on his arm. There was a spot on the upper jaw where two teeth were missing and a corresponding space on his bicep where there was no scar.

"Where did you find this?" Hall asked.

"The day after they found you here, I came to the point. You weren't wearing a life preserver and no one could figure out how you'd gotten this far from the barge without drowning. You couldn't tell us, and I couldn't understand it either."

Hall tossed a piece of driftwood into the water and watched Belker jump in after it.

"Just over there," Silas said as he pointed, "I found a large female dolphin beached on the oyster bar. She hadn't been dead very long and there were no fresh injuries on her body, just an old scar near her pectoral fin. I towed her up to the Waddell Center and asked one of the biologists to see if he could find out what had killed her. When he was finished I asked him if I could have the skull. He cleaned it and bleached it so Gale could put it in her office."

Hall handed the skull back to Silas.

"How did you know?" Hall asked.

"I didn't have any idea until a few days ago. I ran into the biologist when I turned in my tagging log for this year. He told me the dolphin had died from the same chemicals as the fish you and Gale had collected, the same stuff that was on the barge."

Hall thought about the dolphin that used to greet him when he pulled his boat away from his dock. The same one Belker barked at and, he was sure, that Silas had freed from the abandoned fishing net. It all seemed like a long time ago.

"Have you seen the dolphin in the channel going to my house?" Hall asked Silas.

"Not since the storm. I think you should keep it," Silas said of the skull. "It will make for a heck of a story someday when your children ask about it."

Hall agreed.

"I'll bring them here to tell them. It will only take a few minutes to get here from our home on Pinckney Island."

THE END

Acknowledgements

Writing Soundkeeper has been one of the most rewarding experiences of my life. It is the realization of years of dreaming and planning, and the result of many hours at the keyboard. I hope I managed to keep you entertained for at least a little while.

This book would not have been possible without the help and assistance of many others. Any mistakes in the book are the result of my clumsiness and should not reflect poorly on those acknowledged here.

Margaret "Peggy" Van Dyke was my writing teacher and has become a trusted friend and advisor. She read the ugly first drafts and exhausted several red markers with corrections, suggestions, and praise. Through it all, Peggy's encouragement has been unwavering.

When I accompanied Refuge Enforcement Officer Jesse Fielder, of the U.S. Fish and Wildlife Service on patrol, he showed me a side of law enforcement that I had never experienced in my twenty-seven years as a police officer. The men and women who protect our natural resources often work alone in isolated territory, miles from back-up officers. They have my respect and admiration.

Jeroen ten Berge designed the book's cover, and I am grateful for the stunning image he created. I couldn't have hoped for more.

After working with Carin Siegfried, I have a new appreciation for the valuable services provided by a professional copyeditor. Any author who believes they don't need a trained and experienced editor is not serious about their writing. I look forward to working with Carin on all my future projects.

There is only one person who has been there from the beginning. She read the bad writing that wasn't worthy of public consumption, collected the rejection letters that fouled the family mailbox, and dealt with being a writers widow while I flailed away on the computer. When I wanted to quit she wouldn't allow it, and her tolerance and patience for absurd ideas is superhuman. Thank you Joellen. I love you.

Biography

Michael Hervey has been a police officer for over twenty-seven years and was the former outdoors editor for the Stanly News and Press. He lives with his family in the North Carolina piedmont and enjoys all manner of outdoor recreation in his spare time. Banks, the family's chocolate lab, says that any resemblance between him and Belker are completely coincidental.

Please visit
michaelhervey.com
for more information on upcoming releases.

Made in the USA
Charleston, SC
07 July 2013